PROFILES IN CANADIAN DRAMA
GENERAL EDITOR: GERALDINE C. ANTHONY

James Reaney
J. STEWART REANEY

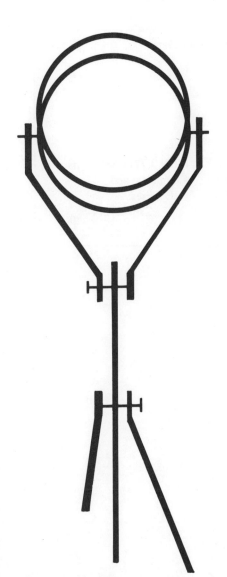

GAGE EDUCATIONAL
PUBLISHING LIMITED

Canadian Cataloguing in Publication Data

Reaney, James Stewart, 1952-
James Reaney

(Profiles in Canadian drama)

Bibliography: p.
Includes index.
ISBN 0-7715-5875-9 bd.   ISBN 0-7715-5865-1 pa.
1. Reaney, James, 1926-   - Criticism and
interpretation.   I. Title.   II. Series.
PS8535.E12Z85   C812'.5'4   C76-017214-5
PR9199.3.R4Z85

123456789 GL 85 84 83 82 81 80 79 78 77

This book is for John Andrew.

Preface

Profiles In Canadian Drama is the first published series of books devoted solely
to Canadian dramatists. The beginning of such a series attests to the fact that
there now exists a solid body of Canadian plays worthy of serious analysis.
Each year additional titles will be published on major Canadian dramatists and
their plays. These analytical studies will be comprehensive enough to include a
short biography, a criticism of the techniques, styles, subjects and philosophies
of individual Canadian playwrights and their plays, and an extensive bibliography. They will be written in a style, which, without sacrificing scholarship,
still will be clear and stimulating enough to capture the interest of the general
reader and theatre buff. We hope that Canadian actors and actresses will also
avail themselves of the opportunity to delve into the background and thought of
the dramatists whose work they bring to life on stage. Certainly the most fruitful
by-product of this series will be the impetus these books provide to read the
plays themselves and to go to theatre to see Canadian drama enacted.

As time progresses, the series will gradually include an ever-increasing
number of Canadian dramatists whose work is compelling enough to deserve
attention. In the final analysis it may be that such a series, taken as a whole and
in retrospect, will embrace not only all the major Canadian playwrights, but
will also spell out for us the inherent qualities of the Canadian people. Writers
today are creating drama revealing the Canadian as the inheritor of so many
diverse qualities and cultures that a national identity could only be revealed in
mosaic. From every province come plays bespeaking the character of that area.
This regional drama at times strikes a universal chord and it is at such a moment
that Canada emerges as a nation. From Newfoundland to Vancouver, the local
playwrights are vividly portraying local people. David French in his two related
plays, *Leaving Home* and *Of The Fields Lately*, offers an honest picture of the
displaced Newfoundlander who brings his wit, his courage, and his colorful
language to the big city of Toronto. Michael Cooke remains with the Newfoundland scene in his attempts to come to grips with the vivid personality of
these seafaring folk. James Reaney uses fantasy and poetic language to reveal
the traits of the nineteenth century Ontario Irish and Scottish forebears of
today's leaders in that province. French Canada has been developing for the

past forty years, a drama which now adequately reveals the typical French Canadian in the plays of such established writers as Gratien Gelinas, Michel Tremblay and Michel Garneau. The West has produced a number of such enthusiastic writers as Sharon Pollack, Tom Cone, Eric Nichols, Tom Grainger, and Sheldon Rosen whose plays are being produced in small makeshift theatres as well as in the established playhouse. ''Social-conscious'' Canadian dramatists are beginning to assert themselves: George Ryga with his concern for the Indian, John Herbert with his sensitivity for the prisoner, David Freeman with his portrayal of the victim of cerebral palsy. Canadian playwrights are delving into the colorful history of Canada and are coming up with such fine plays as John Coulter's *Riel*, where, for the first time since the founding of Manitoba, Canadians gained some perspective on the conflict between the Métis and the Scottish-descended Ontario people as well as their great national hero, Louis Riel.

This volume is a carefully delineated study of the plays of James Reaney, written by his son, James Stewart Reaney, who is very familiar with the plays and their characters as he literally grew up with them. This young writer treats his father's work with an objectivity and clarity surprising in one who has been so intimately and closely associated with them since childhood. It is possible that Reaney, the playwright, saw in his sons and daughter qualities easily transferable to his plays. The element of child-like play and fantasy persists throughout Reaney's work and is one of its outstanding characteristics. These magical and other-wordly aspects serve to convince the audience of truths that are universal.

The author begins by presenting his father—the man and the playwright—in a short biographical sketch followed by a brief commentary on his style in general. There follows an analysis of the plays, beginning with the four schoolplays and continuing through the major dramas to the trilogy, *The Donnellys*. The author reserves until the end, his favorite play and the one he considers the best, *Listen To The Wind*. Frequently alluded to are the Reaney characteristics of freedom and flexibility; originality and creativity. The author has captured his father's spirit in describing his extraordinary imagination, his free association of ideas, his love of names, his brief scenes and abrupt shifts, his penchant for Canadian history and geography, his comic and grotesque characters, his poetic imagery — all of which contribute to making Reaney's free-form theatre the most unique in Canada.

Geraldine C. Anthony, S.C.
Mount Saint Vincent University
Halifax, Nova Scotia

Author's Preface

Right from the opening face-off, I'd like to let you know that this is a book about my father's plays and that I have had a lot of fun writing it. In the writing I have concentrated on the personal contribution of James Reaney to the plays, on the scripts rather than the performances. I have purposefully not included any study of his collaboration with John Beckwith feeling that their lyrical/musical compositions ought to be discussed by someone more confident in his ability to analyse both music and lyrics. Similarly, a definitive work on Reaney's career would have to compare his evolving conception of the theatre with the influences of the three directors responsible for the premieres of most of his plays: Pamela Terry, John Hirsch and Keith Turnbull. The work of the actors, leading up to the formation of the NDWT Company, should also be discussed in a larger context; the changes from amateur to professional theatre and ensemble style from independent companies indicating the changing circumstances of Reaney's theatre. I have chosen instead to focus on the personal aspect of his plays.

The credits and thank-yous involved in this book make it hard for me to believe that any book is ever written alone. The people who helped me are my father, my mother, and my sister; Alvin Lee and Ross Woodman for their inspirational and instructive books on James Reaney; Ted Fulcher for typing so much of the manuscript; John Beckwith for his assistance with *Night-blooming Cereus* and suggestions in general; my friends in Peterborough, London and Toronto for their encouragement and advice; my professors at Trent University; my typing teacher and classmates; my editors, Geraldine Anthony and Conrad Wieczorek for their generous confidence and patience; and finally the people with whom I live for ink, ideas, paper, typing and tolerance. Thank you.

J. Stewart Reaney
August, 1976

viii

Acknowledgements

We wish to thank the following for their co-operation and for their kind permission to quote copyrighted material:

Macmillan Company of Canada Limited (Toronto) and Mr. James Reaney: quotations from *Night-Blooming Cereus; The Sun and the Moon; The Killdeer; One-man Masque*, all of which appear in the collection *The Killdeer and Other Plays*, © 1962.

new press (30 Lesmill Road, Don Mills, Ontario) and Mr. James Reaney: quotations from *The Easter Egg*; *Three Desks*; *The Killdeer*, all of which appear in the collection *Masks of Childhood* by James Reaney; Brian Parker (ed.), copyright © 1972 by James Reaney.

Press Porcépic Limited (70 Main St. Erin, Ontario N0B 1T0) and Mr. James Reaney: quotations from "The Yellow Bellied Sapsucker" (in *Selected Shorter Poems* © 1975), *Sticks and Stones: The Donnellys—Part one*, copyright © 1975.

Talonbooks (201/1019 East Cordova, Vancouver, B.C. V6A 1M8) and Mr. James Reaney: quotations from *Geography Match*; *Names and Nicknames*; *Ignoramus* all of which appear in the collection *Applebutter and Other Plays for Children* by James Reaney, copyright © 1973 by James Reaney and from *Colours in the Dark* by James Reaney; Peter Hay (ed.), copyright © 1972 by James Reaney, and *Listen to the Wind* by James Reaney; Peter Hay (ed.), Copyright © 1972 by James Reaney.

Twayne Publishers Inc.: quotation from p.152 of *James Reaney* by Alvin A. Lee; copyright © 1968 by Twayne Publishers Inc. and reprinted with the permission of Twayne Publishers, a division of G.K. Hall and Co. Boston.

Contents

1

James Crerar Reaney:
Man and Work

James Crerar Reaney was born in 1926 to James Nesbitt Reaney and Elizabeth Henrietta Crerar in South Easthope, R.R. 4, Stratford, Ontario. He received his primary education (1932-1939) a half-mile across the fields at Elmhurst School (which does have several rooms).

The next five years were passed in attendance at the Stratford Collegiate and Vocational Institute. During this time Reaney cycled to Toronto with some friends to see the opening of Walt Disney's *Fantasia*. Also about this time he began to visit his father, who had entered the hospital as an invalid, in London, Ontario. From 1944 to 1948, Reaney was a student of English Literature at the University of Toronto. As an undergraduate, he first published poetry and short stories. The following year he received his Master's degree in English from the University, and won the Governor-General's Award for Poetry for his first volume, *The Red Heart*.

Reaney then began teaching at the University of Manitoba, and continued to do so, with one sabbatical, until 1960. In 1951, Reaney married Colleen Thibaudeau, a poet and fellow student at the University of Toronto. Their first child, James Stewart was born in 1952, and a second son, John Andrew, was born two years later.

One of Reaney's strongest memories from this period is the tent that housed Stratford's opening seasons of Shakespeare. On a pitch-black night, he and Colleen, Pamela Terry, and John Beckwith all bicycled back to the South Easthope farm.

The family returned to Toronto in 1956 as Reaney worked on his doctoral thesis, ''The Influence of Spenser on Yeats,'' under the supervision of Northrop Frye, while also taking a course on Archetypes in Literature from Dr. Frye. At the end of the two-year sabbatical, Reaney was awarded his doctorate in English Literature, and published *A Suit of Nettles* for which he won his second Governor-General's Award for Poetry (1958).

Susan Alice Elizabeth, a daughter, was born in 1959. The Reaney family moved from Winnipeg to London, Ontario, in 1960, with Reaney's acceptance of a teaching position at the University of Western Ontario. This year also marked the premiere of *The Killdeer* (directed by Pamela Terry in Toronto), and *One-man Masque* (Toronto) as well as the first live performance of *Night-blooming Cereus*, which had previously been broadcast by the CBC. In 1962, Reaney received his third Governor-General's Award for the publication of *The Killdeer and Other Plays* and *Twelve Letters to a Small Town*. The same year, *The Easter Egg* premiered in London and Toronto (directed by Pamela Terry). *Names and Nicknames*, directed by John Hirsch, premiered in 1963 (Winnipeg). Two years later, *The Sun and the Moon* had its first performance, directed by Keith Turnbull, in London, Ontario. The same summer Reaney busily prepared three marionette plays for the Western Fall Fair: *Applebutter*, "Little Red Riding Hood," and "Aladdin and the Magic Lamp." Greg Curnoe designed the marionettes and sets for "Little Red Riding Hood," creating a memorable u.s.a. imperialist wolf. Another London artist, Jack Chambers, later filmed the production. With the help of friends, Reaney constructed the marionettes for the other two shows, rather more successfully for *Applebutter* than for "Aladdin and the Magic Lamp" (the genie, himself, was especially poverty-row). In 1966, Reaney directed the first performance of *Listen to the Wind* as part of an all-Canadian season at the Summer Theatre in London. At the Avon Theatre *Colours in the Dark* premiered the following year, directed by John Hirsch, as part of the Stratford Shakespearean Festival's centennial season. Centennial Year also marked the continuing development of the Listener's Workshop in Alphacentre, a community artistic project, wherein Reaney served as a director. At Christmastime, he rented a local theatre to present the plays worked up by this collaboration. *Geography Match*, originally intended for Stratford, instead premiered in the same year, in a production supervised by Reaney, starring students from the neighborhood school. After the activity of 1965-67, the Reaney family moved to Victoria, British Columbia for a one-year sabbatical. At this time *The Donnellys* was researched and partially written. *Sticks and Stones* (1973), "The St. Nicholas Hotel" (1974) and "Handcuffs" (1975) were produced in Toronto, directed by Keith Turnbull. *The Donnellys* remained Reaney's chief dramatic preoccupation, and in Halifax, during the summers of 1973 and 1974, he supervised workshop preparations for the Toronto openings. At this writing the Reaney family resides in London, Ontario.

Since this is a book about the plays of James Reaney, a playwright who feels comfortable with the free-wheeling study of his drama, I feel justified in presenting it in this way. His plays have proceeded from a formal preoccupation with the regeneration of theatre in Canada, through the force of poetic language, to a freer sense of "play" which may include topspinning, mime, marionettes or song as part of the communication.[1] It is not my intention to evaluate this shift in terms of bad to good, or sickness to health, but simply to suggest the reason for the transformation, and also the implications for the future of Reaney's art. At this point, it would probably be fair if I were to include a little of my own collection of significant moments in Canadian drama, tucked into a mathematical grid:

(1947 DDF::Yvan::*The Imperialist*::"The Female Consistory of Brockville")

In order to fit Reaney's work into some kind of context, I think it's important that we record some significant moments in the history of Canadian Drama. This set of four random elements may be decoded as:

1947 DDF to mean: in this year, two acts of Molière edged out among others, William Saroyan, Merrill Dennison (*Brothers in Arms*), Luigi Pirandello, Helen Jerome (*Jane Eyre*) and Noel Coward (*Blithe Spirit*, and *Ways and Means*) for the top award in the Dominion Drama Festival.
Yvan to mean: the fabulous goal scored by Yvan Cournoyer of the Montreal Canadiens in the 1971 semi-finals. Cournoyer scooted in alone on Cesare Maniago, kept closing in, and then suddenly switched from shooting left-handed to shooting right-handed; Maniago froze and Cournoyer put a perfect shot into the top corner. Danny Gallivan was ecstatic.
The Imperialist[2] to mean: a 1904 novel by Sara Jeanette Duncan, about the fortunes of a young man in Brantford, Ontario at the turn of the century. Speeches and ideas are all there, and why isn't it on the stage by now?
"The Female Consistory of Brockville" to mean: The event was the ousting of the town's minister by pressure from a body of church women. As far as the ladies are concerned, the minister is an irritating man with an insufferable attitude toward women. They would like the power to decide for themselves who will run the church and, more particularly, in what manner. The unco-operative cleric must be removed, and the obvious and easy way to do this, considering the precarious nature of a churchman's position, is to start a slander campaign against him. Malicious gossip quickly produces the desired effect and he is ostracized by most of the good people of the town for being a cruel wife-beater and a very unchristian man. However, the proud minister refuses to leave town as expected . . . [3]

Suppose my four choices were to be labelled "Toward a Theory of Canadian Drama," what would they signify? In one way, only that tastes differ as to what is significant. In another sense, however, the set of four is an example of the histories we each could be collecting, beyond that of the drama we find around and within our own lives.

For this reason, the four choices are not quite as random as they appear. The 1947 Dominion Drama Festival would be simultaneous with Reaney's undergraduate years at the University of Toronto. How would the triumph of Molière affect the aspirations of Reaney as a dramatist? The DDF symbolized amateur theatre in Canada, and yet was dominated by foreign adjudicators, foreign scripts, foreign standards, (how to compete with everyone from Molière to Saroyan). Cournoyer is admittedly diversion, but *The Imperialist* is one of the definitive recreations of life in Souwesto (Southwestern Ontario) filled with American annexationists, confused loyalists, politics, love, the beautiful countryside. Anyone familiar with the plot of Reaney's *The Sun and the Moon* will recognize the similarities to ''The Female Consistory of Brockville,'' and it is illuminating to think of the women in Reaney's work as a tribal matriarchy, determined to push out Francis Kingbird on the most spurious of charges.[4] As a result, we find ourselves in a unique position; by including more material in our open-ended set of Canadian drama, we do not only develop a theory. The collection extends in all directions and begins to apply itself to the authors in the country. By collecting a list of Canadian *things*, we have started to discover the hidden history of Canadian drama, and really have started to write our *own* Canadian plays.

An extension of this theory—everyone making lists, plays, gardens, games —is that local regional culture achieves an unprecedented importance. What is happening within the local/regional society is as significant as what is happening in London/Rome. Again, this logically develops into an insight to the plays James Reaney has been writing. Reaney almost invariably keeps the setting of his plays away from Toronto, the centre of his province. Instead of gravitating toward the opportunities of the big city, his characters are always in flight from its perils and madness. The action in many of the plays stays within the bounds of one village, or one farm, somewhere in Perth County. Reaney describes the landscape of his sacred county as faithfully as Duncan records the world of the Brantford town square in *The Imperialist*. ''Toronto'' is reduced to a witch's castle (*The Sun and the Moon*) or a discordant nightmare (*Colours in the Dark*). Such deliberate rejection of the ''city,'' supposedly the centre of the action, places Reaney theoretically at odds with one of the major developments in contemporary Canadian drama. Despite his nationalism, it is difficult to imagine Reaney ever agreeing with this statement:

> Now, if anyone seriously interested in drama wants to learn and work, he can go to Toronto or Montreal. The alternate theatre is booming. I don't dig this idea that he is helped by nourishing his Little Theatre activities out in the Mid-West somewhere. If he really wants to do something, he must pack up and go to the place where the theatre is happening. It's simply like having to go somewhere else to attend medical school . . . [5]

Reaney suspects that Toronto is reducing the rest of English-Canada to an intellectual and artistic hinterland. Not only Reaney's scripts, but also his use of amateurs, simplicity of props, the extreme naturalism of his lighting, his children's workshops, his participation in the planning of the all Canadian summer season in London, Ontario, 1966 — all these reflect a deep rooted animosity toward the character and apparatus of theatre in the big city. Were it not for the success of *The Donnellys* at the Tarragon Theatre, Reaney's position in the Canadian theatre might have remained as an odd paradox. On the one hand there is a strong small town provincialism ("Toronto" as foreign, evil) and on the other hand there is a theoretical sophistication (the determination to produce Canadian culture independent of colonial or international interference).

With the success of *The Donnellys*, however, this position has become even more paradoxical. Reaney, champion of the provinces, reached the height of his popularity with Toronto audiences and critics with a trilogy narrating the life and death of the family in the greatest Souwesto folktale of them all — the Donnellys and the Biddulph horror. Whether this will encourage him to pack up and leave for medical school or not, remains to be seen. While it is true that one of the causes of provincialism is envy of life in the city, it is hard to imagine James Reaney giving up his provincial identity — small-town doctor, or no, to use the medical analogy — to start over again as a dramatist in the big city.

In this introductory chapter I have attempted to provide a model hinting at a useful approach to the study of drama in Canada and perhaps helpful for an understanding of the theatre of James Reaney. One might hope that if we keep building up patterns of Canadian identities, the eventual result will be a fuller impression of the society in which we live and a sense of why it is we want to live in it.

Reaney's drama is now a part of the new Toronto theatre where this kind of building, collecting and comparing of patterns has begun to unfold with force. Audiences wait for a new production of the Factory Lab, David French, Theatre Passe Muraille, David Freeman with the same anticipation with which they look forward to a novel or book of poems by Margaret Atwood, an album by Bryan Ferry, or a film by Claude Jutra. There is a feeling here, akin to what it must have been like to have been a part of rock'n roll in Liverpool about 1960, or a part of films in France a few years before that. For audiences, actors, writers, critics, there is a sense of vitality, life captured for a moment and endlessly new possibilities and beginnings, everyday.

Notes to Chapter One

1. What I have described here is both the development of Reaney's career and his growing personal involvement—through workshops, direction of artistic centres—with drama. The movement from poetry to plays suggests an entry into the public arena to begin with, hence the preoccupation with language. At the height of his personal involvement in the theory and practice of his evolving conception, Reaney seemed to feel that his interest in poetry had been extinguished by his drama (1965-68). See the Conclusion for more on this evolution.

2. Duncan, Sara Jeannette. *The Imperialist*, (Toronto: Copp Clark, 1904).

3. Edwards, Murray D. *A Stage in our Past*, (Toronto: University of Toronto Press, 1968), pp. 131-32.

4. Murray Edwards speculates further as to the identity of Caroli Candidus, the pseudonymous author of ''The Female Consistory of Brockville.'' He remarks that it may have been the ousted minister, a Mr. Whyte, himself. Imagine Francis Kingbird writing a play to clear his name from the slanders of Shade and Moody!

5. Lee, Betty. *Love and Whiskey*, (Toronto: McClelland & Stewart, 1973), p. 301. The remark is attributed to Mr. Tom Hendry.

2

Schoolplays

The collection *Applebutter and Other Plays for Children*[1] offers the most basic approach to the kind of theatre James Reaney wants to develop. These four plays use the characteristic preoccupations and structures of his drama on a reduced scale, allowing an entry into his other work through their simpler forms. Reaney consistently has examined a few themes in his plays, and the value of this collection is that each selection presents a particular, but not exclusive, examination of one special theme. *Applebutter* itself is a Reaney miniature uniting social and personal history with imaginative and mythical elements. *Geography Match* expands the mythic framework in order to depict a personal vision of Canada. The strength of family and community is the foundation of *Names and Nicknames*, a play inspired by wordlists from school spellers. *Ignoramus* discusses the issues of education and maturity in a setting that is knowingly "academic." If the collection were edited together, as this compression of themes suggests, one big play would emerge . . . "You can watch somebody grow up" [p.9] in Canada. A new unity would be formed drawing together spanking, Nanabozho, skipping, *The Little Engine That Could,* factories, *Cours Moyen* . . . a unity that continues in the adult theatre's potential one big play about all of life in Canada.

Reaney has discussed his child drama as a whole in terms of the compositions for children's orchestra written by Carl Orff. In Orff's music, the steady interplay of simple elements reaches a final complexity that the children would not achieve without basic co-operation. A similar procedure is followed in these plays for children. A certain world has been created for children illuminated by continual games, chants, improvisational catalogues, and youthful character types. Children are encouraged by these techniques to bring the energy and culture of their "play" into a more formal structure: not to reproduce adult theatre in a small or even charming way, but to revitalize and direct, perhaps to recall the child in the adult. In this regard, one is struck by the natural fashion by which Reaney is able to place two recurrent concerns (the difficulty of maturing and the importance of community) at the heart of *Names and Nicknames*, a drama for children. At first little Baby Two is able only to gurgle at Grampa Thorntree, "Mooly moo dirly dirly a doidle" [p. 133]. Two pages later, he proudly joins in the defence of Brocksden with shouts as far removed as "Norman" and "Dionysus." Adult heroes may struggle for two acts (at least) before rejecting evil so wholeheartedly. In the childrens' plays though, such wild and optimistic spontaneity is part of the game, and therefore part of the play.

Applebutter combines this spontaneity with details familiar in many of Reaney's longer plays and uses them in marionette form. *Applebutter* tells a Souwesto folktale built around such constants as a child alone, an isolated farmhouse, a sinister hired man, mythical natural forces, and an affectionate presentation of life in Perth County. Quite in keeping with the author's insistence on simplicity is the rough-hewn appearance of the marionettes. They are all primitively formed creatures of wood, bone and string and *not* particularly human.[2] The storyline is similar: a strong and natural focus of attention completely shaped by the hobbit-like pertness of the hero and the power and wisdom of his friends. If there is a Reaney play that does not become melancholy (although Moo Cow mourning the transformation of her sister Tilly into a bottle of Bovril or perhaps a Gladstone bag is glum to be sure), *Applebutter* is it.

What is characteristic of Reaney, even in this apparently casual work is the connection made between social and historical details and personal style. The one act is a glimpse of Perth County enjoying the pleasures of King Pedro and Temperance wine, forever contending with small troubles, yet always well protected by its guardians. Reaney uses conventions and characters true to rural life and folktales to express his personal themes concerning the natural conflict between fertility and sterility, good and evil.

Victor Nipchopper is a character typical of this coincidence of convention and insight. Nipchopper, the hired man, is Applebutter's bitter enemy, and represents the Clifford Hopkins/Bethel Henry/Cousin Douglas "cowbird" villain. Although he is clumsy and oafish, solely capable of mischief and cruelty, he nearly takes Hester Pinch's farm for his own. He bullies and dominates Pinch and Solomon Spoilrod and effectively prevents their marriage and reconciliation with Butter until Moo Cow blasts him right out of Perth County and the play. Indeed, the somewhat enforced betrothal of the quaint couple, Spinster and Schoolmaster, does bring *Applebutter* to a proper conclusion, similar in form to most Reaney comedies. Marriage is an institution that is symbolic of stability and fertility in these works, the image and expression of a society in harmony. It is the intervention of the nature spirits that makes possible this social harmony. Rawbone and Treewuzzle are sensible guardians for Butter and even manage to temper his joking. For Reaney they embody the contemplative good sense of his other heroic figures of good and are the true leaders of the community. They are natural characters in folktales, able to guide and educate Butterkin, majestic but still funny and approachable, like Treebeard in *The Lord of the Rings*.

At heart, though, is the personality of Applebutter. Robust and good natured, he is the "human" character closest to the natural champions. In the process of growing wiser, Applebutter lives up to his extraordinary name; apples into something else delicious; nature and culture, Wuzzle and Perth County at once.

No single schoolkid in *Geography Match* is as lovingly developed as is Applebutter and the cast is instead a composite of children's moods: adventurous, wise, weak, petulant, resilient. The child-actor types mix school contests with archetypal drama in a freely-formed depiction of Canadian identity. For this reason, *Geography Match* closely resembles *Colours in the Dark*, and is separate from the Perth County cycle of plays. It places the journey of the larger work in a different, more hopeful context. The danger in *Colours in the Dark* is that the sick child, alone in the darkened room, will fall out of the dance of life, while the schoolchildren in *Geography Match* are not faced with death or isolation. Their race across Canada divides them into competitive groups, and the finish brings self-recognition, marriage, and co-education.

As theatre, the play develops some of the iconography of *Listen to the Wind* and *Names and Nicknames*. The stream of blue cloth reappears and so does the ladder, symbolic in this play of the trial by pair of stairs that challenges the children. There is a slide, reminding us of the schoolyard, and the fish kites (or spawning salmon) forming a complement to the fish mime at the crossing's start, and a contrast to the children who are completing their quest by travelling to the sea, the home of the salmon.

The geography match near the beginning provides a privileged moment typical of Reaney's plays for children. It places a classroom competition (the match) into the realm of poetic national identity (Canadian place names), without damaging the schoolyard "play" of the contest. Here is an epic fragment revealing the unaltered convention and document as the inspirational source for drama and myth. In the ideally imaginative schoolground of *Geography Match*, the match and these few props are sufficiently powerful to invoke Canada.

The play treats Canadian reality as a complex to be considered in several ways. Icebergs, muskeg, and mountains are given personalities; the place names live with imagination. Our history is handled with devices ranging from Miss Weathergood's wonderfully bad ode upon her home to the ironic humor in Techumseh's remark that "the souvenir business can be carried overly far."[p. 75] to the profound depths of myth and legend as Nanabozho awakes:

> Not since the day I fought with my father the cruel West Wind who killed my mother Loonwater have I felt so wide awake. Children with pure living hearts have awakened me.
>
> [p.77]

English Canadian society is simply, but effectively, analysed in a comparison of Anglican and United Church values, and in the class nattering related to the religious differences. Ultimately *Geography Match* transcends contemporary Canada to narrate the cosmic struggle of light and dark. Weathergood and Wolfwind, who start the race with their bet, are revealed as Coyote and Grizzly Bear of native legend fighting their mythic battle over day and night in Kicking Horse Pass. Everyday aspects of this battle divide the schools into contrasting zones of modern and mythic Canada. The Blazers line up with Wolfwind and strikebreaking, bonds, the United States. The Shady Hillers are backed by Miss Weathergood and side with heroic New France, the fishermen, and Tecumseh. In this way the identity of Canada emerges as the mysterious hero-figure of *Geography Match*: the churches, cultures, histories, geographies, even light and dark are all facets of the national image that are studied during the journey.

While the question of national identity is not answered directly, there is a clear sense of rebirth and new purpose in the lives of the characters. The school children follow an archetypal path across Canada, finally reaching the cave of Grizzly Bear (or the Minotaur's lair). They escape by winding in one child's spoolknitting (or ball of string) and with the help of Miss Weathergood/Coyote discover new identities for themselves. Each child reveals its essential nature in a personal animal riddle which is both a disguise and an emblem. Even the weaker children (sulks or bullies) who find themselves to be a skunk or a mouse secure new strength in the protective and adaptive powers of their animal incarnations. *Geography Match* ends optimistically with the Canadian child able at last to climb the pair of stairs. Then the spoolknitting pulls in a member of the audience, uniting the spectators and players, and suggesting that such exploration and discovery is accessible to anyone choosing to start across Canada.

Little geographic movement occurs in *Names and Nicknames*. The play takes place in one pastoral and idyllic community in Perth County (Brocksden c. 1900). Reaney limits the scope of action for purposes of thematic immediacy, and the title makes the conflict immediately apparent. There is a changeless farm ("Long ago, long ago on Farmer Dell's Farm") [p. 138] and a timeless schoolground. Farmer Dell and his family, farmhands, animals, and fields are part of the world of "names": orderly, vital, fertile. They typify rural innocence and are also characteristic of the strong creative families so important in Reaney's vision. The farm encompasses a universal variety of experience within its hope-filled boundaries, whether it is the cows patiently changing their paths or harvest time or the christening of a child. This is the named cosmos; a world of order and good purpose.

In the same way, the schoolground is a familiar and typically complex setting. When the children are playing their skipping games or making poems out of their readers, they are creating spontaneous, beautiful form — the "plays" mentioned in the introduction. However, when they are worried about appearing too girlish/boyish, or building a snowman, then making the sulky decision to smash him to bits they are succumbing to destructive impulses: in short, to "nickname."

The source of the nicknames is Grampa Thorntree, a malevolent old fence viewer and trapper. Thorntree enjoys the pain and confusion of others, and is at the height of his powers during the winter when he traps at will, ("Rabbit foot not so lucky eh?") [p. 129], walking freely on his snowshoes. His vicious attacks on the names chosen for infant children mean there are "fifty unchristened babies" [p. 129] in the Brocksden neighborhood. Ironically, it is the schoolchildren themselves who are partly at fault for Thorntree's cruelty:

> Haw haw haw. Old Mister Thorntree
> Swallowed a peck of rusty nails
> Spits them out and never fails
> To make them twice as rusty —
> To make them twice as rusty . . .

[p. 111]

These playful, thoughtless taunts arouse Thorntree's hatred and he becomes a bitter enemy of all children. The old man shows real cunning in dissecting the children's fears, with specially nasty attention to youthful boy/girl uncertainty. Thorntree's favorite trick is cursing an infant just prior to baptism with a malicious nickname, maiming the baby for life. A further irony in Thorntree's role is that this nickname would replace the child's true name only if other children chose to follow his example. He can articulate the bad feelings of a community, but he does not need to invent them.

Thorntree is finally overwhelmed by the community of Brocksden as the Dells fight his nicknames under the patient and loving supervision of Reverend Hackaberry. After two Dell children have gone unchristened — for fear of Thorntree's vitriolic tongue—a third child is born and christened in spectacular fashion . . . with hundreds of names. The cast chant and shout the epic list and the old trapper dissolves as a human being. His passing into an actual thorntree is the "awful miracle" Hackaberry had predicted, and recalls the self-immolation of Krook in Charles Dickens' *Bleak House*.

Names and Nicknames concludes with a corresponding sense of jubilant affirmation. The christenings of the Dell's children and the engagement of Rob and Etta, events that had been delayed by Thorntree's curses, join the worlds of farm and school (where Rob had been a nature student) in celebration. Their victory is parallelled by the seasonal changes recited in choral verse that have framed the farm (and the play) with spring, summer, fall, winter, and then the infinite growth of spring. Thorntree has been the winter spirit in Brocksden, a human aberration, yet in character, as a tree, a natural object. His transformation resembles the seasonal change from winter to spring in that his greatest strength is also his fatal weakness. Winter may still life on the farm for a time, but must accept the cyclical pattern of new growth and regeneration. So, with Thorntree: he perversely had been able, while human, to change the very names in the community to his purpose. However, Thorntree is defeated by the sheer variety of these names, of language, and is exiled from the community he attempted to destroy. The optimism of *Names and Nicknames* allows us to reconcile the awful miracle with the newly-strong community. Amid the celebrations of marriage and children—of fertility and order—Thorntree and the disorder and sterility (hurting babies with names) he represents are distinctly marked as a force that is not truly human.

Names and Nicknames is of major significance in the overall pattern of Reaney theatre. It indicates a break with *The Killdeer* and *The Easter Egg*. Dialogue and style of language (virtually all-important in the earlier works) begin to settle back into a new naturalism as choral verse, mime, gesture and chants are used to build up the playworld. There is a feeling of liberation and free play, of childhood and contemplation in the farmyard chores and schoolyard games. For the first time in a Reaney play, verse and dramatic movement operate together in a steady, peaceful process growing outward to unite "turkey in the straw" planting, dancing cowpaths, winter stars, the harvest into one free time.

Ignoramus is another play focussed on the classroom. The situation of the children here is unique. The emphasis is more didactic than *Names and Nicknames*, and more intellectual than *Geography Match*. Children grow up in *Ignoramus*, but do so in artificially controlled environments created by opposing states of mind. So, twenty little orphans float into the modern world, guided by two bitterly opposed educational theorists, Dr. Hilda History and Dr. Charles Progessaurus. Hilda represents the values of traditional schooling, and Charley, the forces of progressive education. Reaney had already examined the controversy in the July Eclogue of *A Suit of Nettles* with Anser assuming the Progessaurus position, and Valancy anticipating the role of a less astringent Hilda. Anser scoffed at the useless nature of Valancy's studies as a gosling (including the sisters of Emily Brontë and the wives of Milton), and argued that the "self" alone was worth teaching. The initial debate in *Ignoramus* reaches a more forceful conclusion. History literally knocks Progessaurus down with her mammoth primary reader in a mock duel:

       . . . Progessaurus:
    Well, I think that a little first book for a first little
    mind should have a little tittle—er I mean a
    little title: Mary, John and Peter?
    Group:
    To which Dr. Hilda History said:

History:
My first reader is called:
Eloise, Vercingetorix, and *Saint* Peter.

[p. 152]

This basic antipathy between Hilda and Charley—the bible versus technology—continues from public forum to personal society, and the marriage that ends the other comedies seems unlikely. What would History and Progessaurus ever manage to talk about?

After Hilda's victory in the duel, both theorists are unexpectedly given the opportunity to raise ten orphans each under the patronage of a wealthy brewer, Mr. Fotheringale. They leap at the chance—and one feels it must be partly to avoid each other for seventeen years. The division of the children into these two groups represents a graphic and satirical extension of both theories in a series of contrasting scenes. Not only do we see first a traditional, then a progressive educationalist at work but we also see into the minds of History and Progessaurus. The two educational societies are expressions of their respective visions of idealized childhood, and of their peculiar worlds.

The actual location of the two schools furnishes the basic design of the production. Charley and his kids, unable to cope with Bruce's hostility wander around and around their island's shoreline, going in circles and getting nowhere until Beatrice intervenes. They are castaways co-operating aimlessly under the supervision of Progessaurus. Indeed, only Beatrice's clandestine adventures with reading look forward to a future for the island children. For History and her children the opposite is true: the limitless possibilities of the prairie horizon and the night sky correspond to the society she is building out of the flood. Love and structure (embroidery, constellations, mothers and fathers) are set against the fashionable wooziness of Progessaurus (fingerpainting, *The Little Engine That Could*, child psychiatrist). Within the motif of the circle (Progessaurus) against the line (History) are the lessons and actions of the maturing students. Form (geometry, grammatical structure, ''The Hummingbird,'' the waltz) with Hilda, versus energy (chemistry, self-expression, ''The Tyger,''[3] twisting the night away) with Charley. The ultimate futility of Charley's approach is apparent in the ironic image of his well-adjusted young drivers, roaring around and around their test track.

Amazingly enough the result of the competition is a tie. Charley really ought to lose, for the childrens' sake if not his own, but Beatrice (the third educational force in *Ignoramus*) redeems him. While keeping her distance from Charley's dubious successes with reverse psychology, Beatrice conducts the true education of her tribe. Acting as a priestess, she has brought forth—unbeknown to Progessaurus—a religion from discarded Bon Ami cans, complete with litany as follows:

Bon Ami
Polishes as it cleans
Makes porcelain gleam
Ne Rougit Pas les Mains

Mode D'Emploi
Directions

No Red Hands
Nettoie les fenetres
N'a pas encore engratigne
Hasn't scratched yet

Polie tout en nettoyant

[p. 195]

This sequence forms a complex capsule definition of Reaney's drama for children. At once moving and self-mocking, the ritual chant expresses his Blakean compression/expansion of the universe into a Bon Ami can. The transformation of the cleaning instructions into Scripture goes further than it might as a "found poem." Instead, there is a discovery and acceptance of the theatre in our lives, in which the structure of the artifact becomes the structure of the drama.

The judgement handed down by the Governor-General—the second wise old man to enter the childrens' lives — is fair to both parties, although his crucial word on the whole experiment is "fanatic." In four set-pieces, two students from each school appear before the Governor-General in a trial of manners, character and worth. The four children, Stephen and Cynthia for Hilda, and Bruce and Beatrice for Charley are by turns exasperating and refreshing. Bruce may be Progessaurus' ideally self-expressive scholar, and Stephen, a model young preppy, but neither is a particularly attractive young adult. The charm and art of Cynthia compensate for Stephen's priggishness, while Beatrice and her existence poem ("love and patience *do* quite change the scene") balance the transistor enforced isolation of Bruce. Thus, *Ignoramus* ends with a delayed ending—in keeping with the artificial nature of the contest. There will be a tie breaker: an exchange of classes.

The Governor-General even speculates that History's students who must now suffer Progessaurus for a year may successfully change *him* despite his trendy ignorance. Then one final turn! As the curtain falls, Bruce drops to his knees, acknowledges *his* ignorance, and begs Hilda History to teach him how to read. The real victory has already been won, though. Through the faith and imagination of Beatrice the children have changed the desert island where they found themselves marooned with Charley into a meadow green and plentiful. Their education is essentially complete, and their minds fully sown.

The four children's plays offer us marionettes and myths, Canada and community, family and education generously reflected in the style of an author who constantly writes for and about children. To really enjoy them, however, both for themselves and as preparation for the "adult" works, I think we should pretend that, like the four friends at the start of *Listen to the Wind*, we are all children in Canada somewhere, thinking about putting on a play. For Owen and his cousins it was to be *Tarzan and the Apes* first, then a "Melodrama"; and for the children in our neighborhood the first idea would probably be Bruce Lee in *Enter the Dragon*,[4] or maybe the way Dave "Tiger" Williams dances after a goal. Beyond kung fu fighting, though? As we think of the four children and four chairs in *Listen to the Wind*, we see a possible solution to the problems of producing something energetic for (young) actors, firm in dramatic structure, and interesting to us (i.e., about Canada). Owen Taylor found his own story in an old book, "The Saga of Caresfoot Court," that his father had given his mother before their marriage. The children's plays are inspired by hopscotch, riddles, schooltexts, and by children with the reminder that we can find our own stories all around us, if only we will let them find us.

Notes To Chapter Two

1. Reaney, James. *Applebutter and Other Plays for Children*, (Vancouver: Talonbooks, 1973). Unless noted otherwise, all references are drawn from this edition.
2. Reaney has noted that Applebutter is his favorite character from among his own works because of the [amateur] craft involved: "I built him myself." "Some Questions & Some Answers."
3. Emily Dickinson and William Blake are personal favorites of Reaney's, and both (like the children in *Ignoramus*) are geniuses who flourished in isolation. Hilda's group recites the poetry of total harmony and confluence, while Charley (unwittingly?) leads his students through a celebration of the tiger's demonic energy. The stage direction "A la The Fugs?" for the Progessaurus sequence refers to the Fugs' reading of Swinburne available on ESP-disk 1018. The Fugs utterly capsize Swinburne's pagan delicacy in a tidal wave of syncopation, compensate for the fact that they somewhat mar *their* Blake recitals with inappropriate settings derived from Country and Western music.
4. Clouse, Robert. *Enter the Dragon*, produced by Paul M. Heller and Fred Weintraub, (Hong Kong, 1973).

3

The Killdeer

The change from the plays for children to the first version of *The Killdeer*[1] seems at first complete; simple direct drama, as consciously open and free as any schoolyard gives way to an expansive conception and intricate detail that is somehow compressed into one front room. As I read *The Killdeer*, however, such a change is more apparent than real. At the centre of *The Killdeer* is the story of three children (Harry Gardner, Rebecca Lorimer, and Eli Fay) and their enemies. The grown-up children are more serious and filled with self-doubt than are the growing-up children in the schoolplays, but their story is essentially the same. If Reaney is writing one big play, his characters here are lost in dark enchanted forests, and are beguiled by fairytale villains. The struggle to maintain and recover their innocence while accepting the passing of their own childhood is the same. It is the genre and milieu that differ. For this reason, I would like to discuss the two *Killdeers* both as generally indicative of Reaney's theatre, and also as individual texts. Each has a special quality: the 1962 work is the author's dramatic premiere, and the revision is an interior reflection echoing his own drama.

The Killdeer (1962) originates many of the themes, characters and situations elemental in Reaney's plays. The first appearance of the predominant theme of childhood liberation and enlightenment has already been noted. Children, who are threatened by oppressive parents or parent-figures, their own insecurities, and social constrictions journey from this state of repression to self-knowledge and psychic liberation in a variety of guises. Harry Gardner, the nominal hero of *The Killdeer* is the prototypical late adolescent confronted by this predicament. He is trapped by a smotheringly affectionate mother, personal feelings of inadequacy and a stultifying provincialism that insists he spend his time "usefully" (i.e., work in a bank). Harry finally breaks free of these bonds by fathering an illegitimate child, an act of evil to the forces that have repressed him, and a victory repeated in *The Sun and the Moon* in a somewhat different form.

Harry Gardner and his odyssey (which is perhaps the easiest strand to discuss) should not be isolated from the overall form of *The Killdeer*. His story is placed amid a complex work filled with sensational subplots, ingrown family histories, and the background of a violent, murderous past. These are all familiar characteristics of melodrama. The turn of plot involving the illegitimate child is only one device expressive of Reaney's fondness for primitive, intense drama. The setting and nature of *The Killdeer* fully indicate his desire for a theatre that draws on unrealistic, almost subconscious response. Reflecting this tendency to work against the sophistication of an audience through melodramatic devices, there is a coincident fascination with the macabre and darkly humorous. Occasionally the explosive plot is held up for examination with self-amused relish. So, Madam Fay narrates her tale of the Lorimers' murder and the suicide of her husband, Mr. Fay, in a teasing fashion, as a sales pitch for her cosmetics.

Acting as balance with the violent, destructive turns of the play is an optimism of form emerging through the incredible resolution of the complexity and convolutions. *The Killdeer* ends with a sense of self-recognition and reconciliation only after the unexpected and miraculous intervention of a totally new character, Dr. Ballad. Reaney strives to unite his Gothic vision of life *and* his optimism into the mood of the Romance: a genre in which the actual and imaginary may meet remote from everyday life. The nature of Romance permits a story like *The Killdeer* composed of tempests and calms, separation and escape, magic and spectacle to patiently find its own form.

There actually seems to be a hint early in *The Killdeer* of the particular reason Reaney has chosen this genre. One of the first jokes is an homage to the late Shakespearean romances. Madam Fay cynically doubletalks the all-too-susceptible Mrs. Gardner into the purchase of forbidden cosmetics:

You say your religion forbids face-painting,
But look at Nature, ma'am. Doesn't the maple leaf
Turn red in the fall? God don't like that?
All those pretty fall colours? . . .

[Act I, Sc. i (1962); Act I, Sc. i (1972)]

An echo may be detected here of the debate over nature and art between Polixenes and Perdita in Shakespeare's, *The Winter's Tale*. The allusion also serves to introduce the most striking decision in Reaney's career: his choice of Southwestern Ontario as a setting for this kind of play, and for most of his plays since. Reaney is certainly a regional artist, committed to a nearly anthropological reproduction of local customs, idiom, and conventions. He is critical of the occasionally repressive character of the region, yet his characters do not so much outgrow Souwesto (i.e., retreat to the city) as confront it and contest the sterility that may be found there, and grow, themselves, in so doing. He has steadily explored the possibilities in this superficially limited culture as inspiration for art and life since the opening of *The Killdeer* in 1960.

Reaney has invoked Proust to defend his use of Perth County material in this fantastic manner. Although possibly an anti-critic gambit, this remark suggests the aura essential to his early plays. In the first Reaney plays, there is a sense of the all-powerful joy in the sudden flowering of the ordinary: a killdeer's cry, sunlight on an easter egg set in motion, huge reaches of involuntary memory, complete with plots, voices, houses, people, gardens: all spring into being.

An admirable textual analysis of the first *Killdeer* is found in Alvin Lee's study of Reaney's work. His treatment of the play as a "reworking of archetypal comedy . . . held together by a carefully worked out pattern of interlocking images"[2] is most useful and exploratory. My own analysis is indebted to the direction provided by Professor Lee, but will be considerably contoured.

The characters in *The Killdeer* are withdrawn from everyday life, although they are close to another physical reality. In fact, they are truly in quite the same farmyard as the geese in *A Suit of Nettles*. Almost all the play's imagery can be seen around the farmhouse where my father grew up in South Easthope: the buggy, the dead horse, the killdeer. This familiar setting is developed into a personal world, a version of Souwesto "opened up" in which characters repeatedly discuss themselves in terms of farm (not necessarily domestic) animals. Manatee, the personification of a farm collapsing into death, pointedly offers Harry this choice of occupations:

> But you should decide now whether you'll be
> A shrike, or a song sparrow, a great blue heron,
> Or a silly harmless frog.
>
> [Act II, Sc. iii (1962)]

The women see their actions as those of hens or crows. Eli speaks of himself as a silly trusting gosling pulled under by the snapping turtle, Clifford. (Kenneth is described by Polly in a similar way in *The Easter Egg*.) Madam Fay becomes a wild animal, a fox doubling over its tracks, or a cat with a mouse (this last according to Attorney Jenkins . . . the kind of prosaic animal imagery one might expect of him). The condition of mature experience and independence is compared to a hawk flying up, freed from its hood at last. And the killdeer itself is a powerful symbol of self-sacrifice, protection, and fertility, as Rebecca and Harry "throw themselves" for Eli, and for each other.

Beyond this continuity of comparison and image is a sense of the mental and physical geography of *The Killdeer*. Two farms stand separated by a swamp. One farm, the Lorimers' is healthy and thriving, and the other, the Fays', has fallen into the county of night under the murderous influence of Clifford Hopkins. The farms are bound together by the jealous insanity of the parents and the "blood, blood everywhere." The swamp contains and conceals the true heart of the play.

As the farms stand for opposing life forces in the psyche of the characters, the mysterious swamp becomes the source of a possible union of the oppositions. Somewhere, by the paths of the swamp is the shack where Clifford met Madam Fay, finally to be murdered/mutilated by her. Yet the swamp is also the place where Becky "can feel its damp sweet darkness/Brooding with frogs singing against my face . . . " [Act I, Sc. iii (1962); Act I, Sc. iii (1972)] and where Dr. Ballad assembles his journal. Ballad himself tends the swamp almost as a freedman farmer might, and he emerges from it as the perfect judge of the utility/fertility of the characters' actions. Withdrawn enough from the mutilation to find it similar to grass growing through the dead horse, Ballad as a swamp dweller is involved (and playwright?) enough also to lead the children into their transformation of self.

By comparison, the revised *The Killdeer* (1968) reaches this transformation through much less drastic and abrupt means. In the original, the movement of the play lead to a house of cards/courtroom virtually demanding the sudden appearance of Dr. Ballad to achieve resolution. The sweep of the original is replaced by a subtle inner structure which allows the near accidental strength of Eli to force Madam Fay into retreat:

> . . . Then go out to your car *now* and turn the key, get it started. Drive away. I won't tell anybody who Cliff should have pointed at until the morning. OK, Mother?
>
> [Act II, Sc. V (1972)]

Thus, the new play closes with an end to the hostilities of the second act, *and* also delivers an inverted reflection of Act One. Eli is finally able to reject his mother, thus reversing the earlier show of maternal strength as Mrs. Gardner sent Harry off to Vernelle Coons. So, the new form of *The Killdeer* appears infused with a magical and healing aura. Harry is tied to his mother in the second scene despite his protests, while Harry in Act II, Sc. ii hears only echoes of his mother's voice . . . and then finds Becky. "The Birthday Party" is a hopeful mirror of the original fourth scene. Harry and Becky, acting as friends and parents have replaced Clifford as Eli's guardians. It is not so much a question in the revision as to what has been washed away by the river of time (Frank, Mrs. Gardner, Clifford), as a new uncovering: what is it that has endured, awaiting transformation?

This *Killdeer* retains the Romance qualities of the original, the strong structure, rejection of conventional psychological development, and overpowering sense of reconciliation. Some of the sudden leaps in time and set changes of the original are toned down, and some of the arbitrary flavor may be compromised, but the essential narrative — and the three heroic children — remain unchanged. Harry, Rebecca, and Eli all face enormous difficulties passing between innocence and experience: Harry Gardner must break out of a satiric present, Rebecca Lorimer from a murdered past, and Eli Fay from a timeless nightmare which makes all experience into one dark room alone.

Harry is trapped in a house made of sugar candy (a childish conception of the perfect home) dominated by the will of Mrs. Gardner:

> Harry, I wish you'd come in the back door with your bicycle. If a piece of mud dropped onto this
> Floor I'd skin you.
>
> [Act I, Sc. ii (1962); Act I, Sc. ii (1972)]

He expresses his insecurity in a surge of misogynism and confused despair (qualities also shared by the line of Reaney anti-heroes Harry originates):

> . . . Every Saturday night Mother used to
> Wash me all over. To have a woman know all about you
> From the time you're little! —
> She's even had you in her belly
> . . . One thing I shall never understand.
> How women can give birth to men.
>
> [Act I, Sc. ii (1962); Act I, Sc. ii (1972)]

Mrs. Gardner's fetish for collecting threatens to turn Harry into another ornament in the front room, another China figure (or whatever happened to *Mr*. Gardner?). His job at the bank offers no escape, and his marriage to Vernelle Coons is an even greater trap. As the second act makes clear, this marriage of mutual convenience has been as poisonous in its way as Becky's marriage to Eli. In order to truly escape the control of his mother, it becomes paradoxically evident that Harry must re-enter the front room of his adolescence.

If Harry is a conventionally immature character (a "mama's boy"), Becky is equally restricted by her childhood, but in a less satirical way. Rebecca has survived the murder of her family with an inner beauty and optimism that borders on the totally naive. So, she marries Eli without properly considering Clifford's effect on her own future. Thus, the good intentions of

> . . . love's solution to the puzzle of hatred.
> Eli and I will untie the evil knot.
> Mr. Hopkins will help us both. Thank you.
> I feel very happy . . .
>
> [Act I, Sc. iii (1962); Act I, Sc. iii (1972)]

are compromised immediately by the sinister good cheer of Clifford and Eli's own doubts. Becky later describes her marriage to Eli (and Clifford) as hate-filled. Her goodness and good intentions have not been enough to break the psychic grip on Eli. In this instance, Becky recalls her mother. From the story Madam Fay tells Mr. Budge and Mrs. Delta, we can see that Rebecca Lorimer could not save her foster-sister from Clifford long ago, because her purity left the young Rebecca unable to comprehend the evil in others. Becky is paralyzed in the same way when Clifford suggests to *her* that they run off, leaving Eli alone. At this crucial moment, Becky is able to help neither Eli nor herself. This critical moment of weakness implies incompletion in Becky's character. She needs Harry (who needs her and has fought to free himself from his mother and Vernelle) to help save Eli. There must be mutual love for the solution Becky proposes with such happiness.

Eli faces the most spectral problems on his way out of childhood. Clifford shatters Eli with the enforced discovery of the child's murdered family, and Eli collapses into the arms of his new father/mother. In the second act, he has been healed a little by his summer with Harry and Becky, but his terrified gasps "Don't let her get me" [Act III, Sc. ii (1962)] are surely the reflection of a child's pervasive fear of a hostile adult. Eli is grappling with the false innocence of childhood. The toys he plays with are the nursery room image of his poetic denunciation of clocks, and (actually) his adolescence. It takes all of Harry's and Becky's love to save Eli from his deliberately arrested development (the long scene with Harry recalling "The Fable of the Babysitter and the Baby" from *Colours in the Dark*, and Mitch and Owen discussing "Bottles" in *Listen to the Wind*). All these scenes are healing in their resolve that the characters involved accept some aspect of growing up: death, loss of innocence, sickness. *The Killdeer* ends with Eli healed, and his emergence as a grown-up child. He is the hero of the last scenes of the play, as Harry and Becky are the heroes of the first and middle sections.

Following the three children through *The Killdeer* minimizes the power and importance of Madam Fay. After the death of Hopkins she is the force of evil in the play, determined to reduce Eli completely, hang Becky, and thwart Harry. Her speeches are marked by a theatrical self-consciousness that allows Fay to overpower, even as she bares her secret heart. At the peak of these scenes ("You'd better buy a thing more. I don't usually do that scene. It tires me out . . . ") [Act I, Sc. i (1962); Act I, Sc. i (1972)] is a combination of inner torment and stunning curtain call beg-offs. She plays at Abab in her little pink car and all because (though this is a dangerous word in Romances):

She didn't love me enough even to hate me.
There was this abominable smell. I fell ill.
She slept, but I didn't. I got up and went to her dress.
In the pocket there was still the dead bird.
She'd rather have a dead thing crawling with worms
Than break the shell of evil I lay hatching in . . . .
[Act III, Sc. i (1962); Act II, Sc. iii (1972)]

The notion of her own fragility as a child (the egg) illuminates Madam Fay's demonic obsession. She wants back into the world and time before her foster sister, Rebecca, found the killdeer, with the innocence of that childhood to be somehow regained through the violent annihilation of other children.

The diminished role of Madam Fay in this reading of the revision is justified by the alien quality of her performance in the fairy-tale world built by the children. Clifford and Madam Fay are powerful nightmares, belonging to the confusion of the first act; after the summer together they are only haunting intruders at Eli's celebration:

. . . I'll be the orange devil waiting in the stove
I'll be the chimney trumpeting the night . . .
I'll be the wind moaning in the old pantry
Whistling for some stale pie . . . .
[Act III, Sc. ii (1962); Act II, Sc. iv (1972)]

The play inevitably leads to the "birthday" party and the speeches marking the occasion (vacations or newspapers or Angora bunnies) are serenely concerned with nothing/everything. Eternity is simply there in the front room, part of the possibilities for Harry, Rebecca, and Eli.

The language is at ease in the second act, and the actors communicate more lightly. Harry once felt compelled to crush an egg, to smash the claustrophobic talkersation, and to show that he really lived. In the second act, however, his whimsical plea that the autumn needs a giant outdoor stove to be truly enjoyed typifies the new, free environment. One thinks of the clever footstep mimes, the spinning bicycle wheel (also a transitional device in *Colours in the Dark*), Eli's toys—the signs of his childishness *and* weapons to beat back Madam Fay. All this highly colored activity, the new energy of things and gestures predicts and reinforces the traumatic effect of the bird with the broken wing on Madam Fay. Long ago the killdeer swept Madam Fay apart from her foster-sister, and now she is swept away from her son as he holds out the same bird.

In the introduction to this chapter, I noted the special qualities to be found in each *Killdeer* text, and with this in mind I would like to suggest the special value apparent in studying both works together. The 1960 original and the 1968 revision of *The Killdeer*, considered together, form James Reaney's own commentary on the changing nature of his drama. The design of the revision calls attention to this commentary. By repeating the first act without change, his densely-written predominantly verbal works are represented. As contrast, the second act allows greater freedom of language and action, typical of Reaney's theatre since Listener's Workshop and *Listen to the Wind* (1966). The revised drama serves to unite the two styles into another look at "the story of the two girls and the bird"[3] a singular moment which opens artistic compromise into artistic autobiography.

Notes To Chapter Three

1. Reaney, James. *The Killdeer* from *The Killdeer and Other Plays*, (Toronto: Macmillan of Canada, 1962); Reaney, James. *The Killdeer* from *Masks of Childhood*, edited by Brian Parker, (Toronto: new press, 1972). Unless noted otherwise, all references are drawn from these editions. Written in 1960 and revised in 1968, the two versions were published in 1962 and 1972.
2. Lee, Alvin. *James Reaney*, (New York: Twayne Publishers, 1969), p. 133.
3. Reaney, James. "Author's Note" from *Masks of Childhood*, edited by Brian Parker, (Toronto: new press, 1972), p. 200.

4

One-man Masque
Night-blooming Cereus

Both *One-man Masque* and *Night-blooming Cereus*[1] were performed as part of "An Evening with James Reaney and John Beckwith" in April, 1960. I would like to comment on both pieces as different, but related, aspects of the larger Reaney works that were to follow. The two works pull in opposite directions as *One-man Masque* is cosmic abstract, *Night-blooming Cereus* is intensely local, and unexpectedly concrete. Further, the premiere of *One-man Masque* starred . . . James Reaney as the narrator (implying utter freedom and control of performance), and the libretto to *Night-blooming Cereus* was carefully fitted to John Beckwith's score (implying quite the opposite). *One-man Masque* is markedly influenced by Reaney's reading of William Butler Yeats. *Night-blooming Cereus* is an original fantasia set in Perth County. *One-man Masque* traverses the cyclical funhouse of the mind, while *Night-blooming Cereus* is mostly set in the front parlor of a humble cottage. Both end affirmatively, yet they play differently together.

The stage for *One-man Masque* is not sparsely set: in a way it is as crowded with life and association as is any galaxy. Reaney has divided the stage into two groups of familiar objects depicting the worlds of life and death, arranged in two circles linked by a coffin. Life props are elementary, "simple objects that you find around any house." [*Masque*, pp. 175-76] These include chairs, a table, a bed. The props of Lady Death are of the everyday variety, also: a hall tree, a shoe harp, (eventually a Reaney archetype for the stage), a spinning wheel, a cardboard box. Birth is described with the death props, as the nine months of pregnancy include the hall tree and the big spinning wheel, and a month later, a baby (the smallest chair) is born. The baby is found in the adult world of the bedroom or drawingroom, hardly just escaped the pre-birth world of death. Unlike the life props, the objects in the death cycle (all wooden) are not things with which we grow up. Rather, they are things to which we become accustomed: the spinning wheel with its infinite weaving and unravelling, the decaying box, the mirror that looks back.

The battles of the embryonic child are recounted in the first poem, "The Baby." Aside from the formidable victories, the newborn child brings word of two gifts,

And the darkness gave me
Two boneless wands or swords:
I knew not their meaning then
Whether traps or rewards.
One was the vorpal phallus
Filled with jostling army,
Henhouse and palace
Streetcrowds and history.
Two was the magic tongue
Stuffed with names and numbers,
The string of song,
The waker from fallen slumbers.

[*Masque*, p. 177]

The connection between speech and sexuality, between the act of love, regeneration, and the ''waker from fallen slumbers'' (which is art as well as conversation) informs the rest of Reaney's works. In this case, the child in the womb knows more of its potential for self-identification than do adults, asleep in the fallen world. The vorpal phallus is the sower of future generations, of history, while the tongue is the gift that may rouse the sleepers. Names arrive after the jostling army but the palace needs the conscious string of song to avoid the lapse of history into a henhouse. As the child is born, both gifts are suddenly revealed as impotent. The rest of the life-cycle narrates the maturation of the human in sexual and social terms: childhood, adolescence, marriage, old age. Reaney uses a variety of methods and language to illustrate the multiplicity of this life. Childhood musings and memories in old age are rendered as concrete reflections. Marriage is treated as a recital from the Eaton's catalogue section on wedding gowns. Thus the language contains childlike questions:

Don't you wish that you could have seen a great auk or a dodo? Perhaps when I grow up I shall sail to a place where they still are — around the corner of a cliff — the great auk, over the low sandy hill — on the desolate beach — two dodos.

[*Masque*, p. 179]

to complicated echoes of Spenser:

Then from your hand I took
My ring: from the hag's claw
I took my golden ring,
Her breasts like pigsties.

[*Masque*, p. 183]

and even to realistic snatches of satire:

> I had a friend who said two days before the Conversat: "I haven't got an
> invitation to the Conversat yet, and it's two days to go, but I'm going to get
> one." And she did. I often wonder how she did it.
>
> [*Masque*, p. 181]

Death, the end of the life-cycle, pulls The Scavenger into a coffin and the
work abruptly leaves the familiar diverse surface world for the island of the
unknown.[2]

The violent tumble into the world of death leaves the narrator alone in the
afterlife. At this point, it might be expected that the dead soul would be
consigned to heaven, hell or purgatory. Instead, the soul progresses through
successive stages of adjustment to the afterlife and journeys back to rebirth.
W.B. Yeats outlines the stages at length in *A Vision*,[3] and in his thesis ("The
Influence of Spenser on Yeats"); Reaney summarizes them in these terms:

> . . . In the Meditation (I) the Spirit broods over its last moments. The
> Dreaming Back (II) may become a return. Here one may be reborn into the
> Terrestial Condition in order to relive some particularly knotted piece of
> life and get it right this time. The second stage also contains the Phantas-
> magoria already discussed where emotions and imaginations only partly
> realized in life are here thoroughly expanded and exhausted. Next (III)
> come the Shiftings where the torturer gets the chance to be the person he
> tortured; then (IV) the Marriage or Beatitude where the Spirit sees the
> Celestial Body as a whole, old Husk and Passionate Body completely
> withered away. Surely here is where Yeats would put the escape into the
> thirteenth Cone, if anywhere. It is my impression that the Instructors
> rather hedged when it came to stating precisely how one got into that
> Cone. The next two states are Purification (V) and the last of all
> Foreknowledge (VI). In the Purification the Spirit must substitute for the
> Celestial Body seen as a whole, its own particular aim . . . In the Fore-
> knowledge State, the Spirit completes its vision of its new life and accepts
> it. . . . [4]

The poems and recitals constituting the world of death do not correspond
exactly to this pattern, but it is possible to establish a system of similarities and
parallels. "Death's World" contains some of the brooding of the Meditation:
"The Ghost" is indebted to the concept of the Return, even in the flashback to
the real world:

> Sister Cecilia, the figure in the convent orchard has been seen again.
> Digging where the abandoned well is under the old tree.
>
> [*Masque*, p. 188]

Yeats ascribes compulsive activity such as the digging to the guilty and restless among the dead. The shiftings coincide with the "simple old me," "The Executioner of Mary Stuart," the torturer looking for the woman he killed. Similarly the marriage fits in with "Doomsday." Revelation should open the Spirit to the Cone:

> Trumpet!
> Drummer!
> Thunder!
> Vomit you cannibals!
> Shake out those,
> Those old flesh dresses
> For the resurrection parties and balls!

[*Masque*, p. 190]

Although the grotesque self-description of "The Dwarf" does not sound especially indicative of the state of Purification, it serves a purgative, evolutionary function. Getting smaller; the dwarf is the harbinger of the new contribution, a rough baby edging into the cradle:

> Come here shepherds. Here's the way.
> Bah bah bah for an incarnation.
> This way aristocratic intelligence.
> Meow meow for a new sensation!

[*Masque*, p. 192]

At the close of this diabolical nativity scene, the speaker flies over the water to "The Lost Child," or, in Yeats' terms, the Foreknowledge. The floating child is an archetype in the line of Moses, even the free-floating embryo at the end of *2001*,[5] lost in winter, first of the new civilization:

> I push the shore and kingdom to you,
> O winter walk with seed pod ditch:
> I touch them to the floating child
> And lo! Cities and gardens, shepherds and smiths.

[*Masque*, p. 193]

So, the cycle ends with the speaker alone on a winter walk, all nature withered; he kneels by the cradle, seedpods holding the Christ-child of spring.

Reaney has drawn on *One-man Masque* in later works, particularly *Colours in the Dark*, but has never since presented such a naked definition of life and death. *One-man Masque* defines these terms in a purely abstract fashion. The mental gymnastics and solo daring of the performance combine in a tour-de-force quite unique in his career. For the side of his drama not apparent in *One-man Masque*, it is necessary to turn to *Night-blooming Cereus*, and the guests in Mrs. Brown's front room.

Reaney and Beckwith combine in *Night-blooming Cereus* to compose a new kind of opera: a combination of Charles Ives, Souwesto and originality: in short, the first opera in which everything happened before the curtain went up. Charles Ives is not a direct influence on the music or libretto, except in the use of regional hymn tunes as part of the score. Ives functions instead as an inspirational example, as he boldly composed American symphonies in the midst of European-oriented art, using "Turkey in the Straw" alongside Beethoven. So, Reaney and Beckwith work together in this tradition, striving to create a distinctly Canadian opera, without composing in privacy and isolation as did Ives. The unique Souwesto quality of the opera and its original source, unlike most other librettos which are adaptations, locate *Night-blooming Cereus* as a typical Reaney work. Beckwith supplied metric and thematic contours, and Reaney produced a libretto that reads like *The Killdeer* on a reduced, melancholy scale. What is unique about *Night-blooming Cereus* is its simplicity. This is the one early Reaney work for stage which I would confidently attempt to synopsize.[6] *Night-blooming Cereus* proceeds at the same eccentric pace as *The Killdeer* or *The Easter Egg*. When things do happen, they occur with breathtaking haste. Conversely, when almost nothing is happening, line after line of dialogue gently ripples by in conversations that could resolve themselves in a few tense exchanges.

So, the entire first scene is expositional as Alice seeks to find the address of her grandmother's house. That information, not quick in arriving, Alice receives as an earful of town gossip, memory and pettiness. She does hear of Mrs. Brown's lonely existence, and of the night-blooming cereus—which the audience sees on a magic lantern projection. Scene One dims out with Alice walking on the late March snows of Shakespeare, looking for the humble cottage on Maple or Walnut Street.

Reaney has ingenuously confessed that he did not know exactly what an expositional scene was at the time he wrote this opening, and the result is assuredly open to the charge of amateurish awkwardness. Alice and the two girls ramble along. Why not just give the address and leave it at that? The scene does move slowly—but, it does not lumber about gracelessly, and I think the reason for its extreme relaxation is apparent in the next scene, which features Mrs. Brown in her parlor.

The fifteen minute solo as Mrs. Brown does the dishes, sweeps, rocks, and sings her hymns is quite unexpected in opera: where is the excitement? On reflection, however, we find ourselves examining the household routine in a new, even revolutionary, way.

Night-blooming Cereus focusses, almost microscopically, on Mrs. Brown as she drifts through one of many, many similar days since her daughter ran away.

Here we have the key to the tranquil pace of the opera. If the story were narrated too quickly, it would sound quaint, commonplace. Only through a careful recreation of the Perth County milieu (Scene One) and the life of Mrs. Brown (Scene Two) is the magical resonance of the third scene possible. As it is, the scene with Mrs. Brown is one of the most moving Reaney has written. Old women predominate in his first plays, and Mrs. Brown is profoundly beautiful: Mrs. Gardner in her last years, lonely for her child:

> Whose face appears more often than not
> In the dust and the fire and the knot,
> And the blowing rain on the window
> And the tree-branches' shadow
> Contain your face there! and again there!
> My lost girl in the dust in the air.
> But it is best to go on sweeping
> Over the faces better than weeping.

> [*Cereus*, Act I, Sc. ii]

Mrs. Brown's hymns, like Ives' use of similar melodies, are a touchstone of the ordinary in the unfamiliar. The sharp juxtaposition of the houseplants with the magic of the cereus is a preparation for the evening hymn, which places all of Heaven into the image of an old woman playing her harmonium. Mrs. Brown sings of seven-roomed heaven, in its seventh room ''All children and cousins/ All brothers and sisters/and fathers and mothers/and relatives lost . . . '' [*Cereus*, Act I, Sc. ii] looking forward to the sevens and family pyramids of *Colours in the Dark*. The seven rooms of heaven are also what Mrs. Brown's cottage would be if her daughter should return—should the cereus open. Alice knocks at the door ending the scene, commencing the unflowering.

At first, Mrs. Brown dances away from Alice, afraid that the young woman will vanish:

> Like a snowflake in a stream
> You will disappear.
> As all the other times I've seen
> You, my dear.

> [*Cereus*, Act I, Sc. iii]

Mrs. Brown keeps her distance refusing to touch Alice. The haunting second scene has anticipated this rejection. Everyone of the old woman's household chores has faded into the face that now appears at her door. Fooled by the illusion so often before, Mrs. Brown is unwilling to welcome Alice, and shoos her granddaughter into a corner.

The third scene introduces four new characters — the guests who have come to see the cereus blossom. Mrs. Wool, the telephone operator, is a chatterbox in the line of Budge or Delta. Next is Ben Smith, the storekeeper's son, bored with his indoor life. After Ben, Barbara Croft, the village foundling, arrives, also weary of her lot, sleeping in haylofts:

> *Ben*:
> Not an orphan girl but it would be nice
> To be a blacksmith's orphan apprentice.
> *Barbara*:
> Oh I'd like to be a storekeeper's son all right
> And have food, father and mother, all day and night.
>
> [*Cereus*, Act I, Sc. iii]

The final guest, Mr. Orchard, is able to cure the spiritual ailments of both Ben and Barbara:

> Young man, I need someone turnip rows to scuffle
> And juniper trees to trim and dig up.
> Young girl, I'm sure you could in the greenhouse ruffle
> The sweet smelling rows of white carnations.
>
> [*Cereus*, Act I, Sc. iii]

Mr. Orchard carries a small apple tree, and passes out seed packets to the other characters. Winter is ending soon, and Orchard's gifts are full of hope for a healing spring.

All is tranquil and optimistic for a moment, a mood shattered by the roar of the night train to Toronto. Reaney's extensive discussion of the train casts it as the villain of *Night-blooming Cereus*:

> . . . Cease your dreams. I am (unless stopped for a train strike) that which is. Your plant with its angel flower can't change me. It is, thinks Mrs. Brown, is. It is is. And there's no use trying to shut it out.
>
> [*Cereus*, Act I, Sc. iii]

But, the roaring subsides. The clock stops striking midnight, and, as the mechanical world (train, clock) retreats, the timeless world of reconciliation and self-discovery hovers inside the flower. All the characters sing a hymn to encourage the opening, and during its verses

> This voice is like the south wind,
> My heart is like the snow.

But when I hear its gentle sigh
I feel my winter go.

[*Cereus*, Act I, Sc. iii]

Mrs. Brown accepts Alice. Sadly, Alice relates "I am your daughter's daughter. She died a month ago." [*Cereus*, Act I, Sc. iii] Yet there is still the recognition, the new hope. The guests all await the blossoming of the cereus, and the vision of their lives, past to future. Mrs. Brown and Alice have already opened their own angel flower, filling the room with recognition and love. As the flower's petals do gradually open, there is a joyful celebration by the whole congregation:

When I behold
All this glory
Then I am bold
To cross Jordan.
Open, flower.

[*Cereus*, Act I, Sc. iii]

As with *One-man Masque*, which ends with the candlesticks of Revelations 1:12 – 13, *Night-blooming Cereus* closes on a triumphant note. The pilgrims have gathered within sight of paradise, ready to "end the story."

At the start of this discussion, I suggested that *One-man Masque* and *Night-blooming Cereus* could be read/edited together as related aspects of Reaney's dramatic sensibility. My theory goes something like this.

Reaney's plays use two principles of narrative structure. One is basically linear. The action proceeds along various routes until something revelatory happens. After this revelation (easter egg, cereus, wuzzle, several hundred names) occurs nothing will ever be the same in the community. The other tendency is toward cyclical works, (*A Suit of Nettles*, *One-man Masque*, *Colours in the Dark*). Here, the effort is directed into one circular vision, encompassing all the previous changes. As we read through the combination of *One-man Masque* and *Night-blooming Cereus*, it is possible to foresee an eventual fusion of the two forms.[7] *Colours in the Dark* is thus perceived as an extension of *One-man Masque* in formal terms, influenced by the slides and stage-business of *Night-blooming Cereus*, and using similar Souwesto folktales (Mr. Winemeyer, the endless string) as its basic units. *Listen to the Wind* goes even further than this in binding the two principles. The narrative of that play involves the frustration of a linear story (no revelation for Owen) with the perfectly-formed circular construction of the world below.

So, *One-man Masque* and *Night-blooming Cereus* apparently eccentric, uneasy fifteen-year partners, are to be comprehended as a valuable contrast. In

1960, the circle and the straight line were placed side by side, and it was necessary for Reaney to develop a new model theatre before the two could function uniformly.

Notes to Chapter Four

1. Reaney, James. *One-man Masque* and *Night-blooming Cereus* from *The Killdeer and Other Plays*, (Toronto: Macmillan of Canada, 1962). Unless noted otherwise, all references are drawn from this edition.
2. " . . . opening night was not the calmest night I've lived through by any means. The masque turned out to be ten minutes too long, so I dropped some poems by the way. Getting into the coffin, putting on dark glasses and getting out happened all right. At rehearsal I'd got stuck, and the candles didn't set me ablaze . . . " Reaney, James. "An Evening with Babble and Doodle: Presentations of Poetry" from *Canadian Literature* XIL, (Spring, 1962), p.43.
3. Yeats, William Butler, *A Vision*, (London: Macmillan, 1937).
4. Reaney, James. "The Influence of Spenser on Yeats," doctoral thesis, (University of Toronto, 1958), pp. 192-93.
5. Kubrick, Stanley. *2001: A Space Odyssey*, produced by Stanley Kubrick, (Great Britain, 1968).
6. At the risk of proving myself wrong, here goes: Once upon a time, the daughter of Mrs. Conrad Brown of Shakespeare in Perth County ran off with a man. Mrs. Brown, heartbroken, became a recluse. As the action of the opera opens, Alice, the granddaughter of Mrs. Brown, arrives in Shakespeare searching for the home of her grandmother. For Mrs. Brown, it is a momentous day: she has invited four of her acquaintances over for the evening to watch her night-blooming cereus blossom for the first time in one hundred years. Despite the majesty of this impending miracle, it is clear that Mrs. Brown misses her daughter very much. Yet when Alice arrives at the front door, Mrs. Brown refuses to accept her as being human. Guests arrive for the evening, some content, some discontented. A man called Mr. Orchard offers work at his plantation to the two young guests, Ben and Barbara, and they cheerfully accept, eager for a new life. A train passes by the cottage. The characters are thrown off momentarily and they rally by singing a hymn to encourage the cereus to blossom. As they sing, something happens, and Mrs. Brown discovers Alice as her grandchild. The plant begins to unfold and all the characters sing a hymn for the crossing of Jordan and calling on God.

As may be observed, as much time is passed in setting the scene as in outlining the action.

My comments here and throughout the section on *Night-blooming Cereus* are indebted to the advice and assistance of John Beckwith.
7. Under this analysis, a play such as *Geography Match* is revealed as a complex combination of narrative threads. Here, the action is linear (across Canada), leading to a revelatory struggle (Grizzly Bear versus Coyote for the mastery of the universe) after which the characters are literally transformed. Yet there is an implicit circularity in the action also: as the schoolchildren cross Canada they approach the moment of their rebirth both as animal-humans and as the children of Stuffy-Smith and Birdwhistell. In this case the straight line proceeds to a point where it is revealed as one segment of a larger pattern, the circle. *Geography Match* also provides an interesting example of the manner in which Reaney is able to combine personal imagery with his sense of character. The furry motoring gloves that Mr. Wolfwind wears are not only part of his disguise as Grizzly Bear, they are a direct reference to "The Ghost" in *One-man Masque* as well: a private symbol from an "adult" work used freely in a pageant for children.

5

The Easter Egg

"Another impulse behind the play, and now I branch off into the problems of direction, was to write for Pamela Terry a neat, tidy play, concentrated in time and place, with few characters. My previous play, *The Killdeer* beautifully realised by her, had presented difficulties of too much time, space and character . . . "[1]

"Compton-Burnett's novels examine the theme of Power in a family setting. All her novels are concerned with families. In the family Compton-Burnett sees a fascinating opportunity to describe the effects on human behaviour when seven or fourteen people live too closely together in a country house; how, for instance, some become tyrants, some murderers, some misers, some go mad, and some, although weak . . . manage to keep their character sweet and good."[2]

The Easter Egg[3] resembles a tentative compromise between the compressed world Reaney detects in the Compton-Burnett novels and the neat and tidy promise of his introduction. So playfully determined to maintain the unities of time, place and character is this second play that it qualifies as a tour-de-force in face of realist opposition to *The Killdeer*. True enough, the romance genre of the earlier play is obscured, but the new qualities in *The Easter Egg* bring it no closer to a work of conventional realism. If there is a compromise with the audience evident, it lies in a slight change in overall form. *The Killdeer* (1962) is, in part, constructed around a Gothic mystery (who killed Hopkins? How did Mr. Fay know?). *The Easter Egg* is a different sort of entertainment, more like a thriller: spooky house, mutually suspicious characters, intrigue, a struggle for power. Such an adjustment aside, a hard-core realist is unlikely to be satisfied. The original *Killdeer* asked audiences to not disbelieve some rather elaborate situations, and *The Easter Egg* goes further, goes too far.

There is the notorious instance of the batkilling. As an index of human cruelty, the batkilling is comparable to animal deaths in other Reaney plays (and within *The Easter Egg* to George's killing of Kenneth's cat, Cocoanut). Usually such cruelty is the expression of a hidden evil. Here, the batkilling is colored with perverse sexual overtones and completes the seduction of George

Sloan by Bethel. Psychology, in *The Easter Egg*, reaches the truly absurd with
the success of this seduction. George feels somehow compelled to marry Bethel
because he has killed a bat.

Insane as this compulsion may be, it is the ''natural'' result of the
(Compton-Burnett-styled) setting of the play. Although there are only five
characters present, their relationships are caught in a neurotic and repressed
web. Bethel Henry is the *stepmother* of *both* Polly Henry and Kenneth Ralph.
She has dominated their lives since the deaths of their fathers: Bishop Henry by
lightning and Ralph Ralph (!) by his own hand. Polly has managed to escape.
Kenneth, however, is still imprisoned (as an attic child) by the shock of his
father's suicide, and Bethel's cunning since that time. Bethel met Polly at
college, and as Polly explains:

> I should explain that my home also happened to be a bishop's palace. And
> when father knew that — he'd never met such a charming heathen and so
> close to the palace too. No need to go to Africa. So by slow degrees you
> allowed yourself to be converted and soon you and father were both
> paddling around in the baptismal font. Why I'm your godmother! . . .
>
> [Act II, Sc. v.]

Stepmother versus godmother: family life is forced inward. Even the two
characters outside the houses Bethel has conquered are drawn into the web.
Polly's fiancé is George Sloan, a divinity student (as in *The Killdeer*, a way out
of the small town). George is a secret childhood enemy of Kenneth's, and it was
at Bethel's suggestion that he killed Cocoanut, some fourteen years before:

> When that kitten disappeared Kenneth really went crazy. It most made for
> his breakdown.
>
> [Act II, Sc. ix]

Ira Hill, the local doctor, has been a lover of Bethel's *and* a friend of Polly
and Kenneth. He sides with Polly, and against George and Bethel, over the
chance of recovery for Kenneth.

Here, as in the style of *The Killdeer* is an interior design which allows the
story of Kenneth's recovery to be read several ways. To Bethel, Kenneth and
his enclosed childhood is a minor chapter in the novel Ira calls:

> . . . The Bethel Story!
> One: comes down from the mountain
> Two: scrubs the professor's kitchen
> Three: scrubs the professor in his tub
> Four: Kenneth's father blows his head off

Five: Comes into Kenneth and also money
And house and estate and status and —

[Act I, Sc. ii]

The day of the play is crucial in the slambang rise of this heroic tyrant from the kitchens to the head of the household. Bethel is planning to give a dinner party for the university élite, an event that will mark her acceptance by the most exclusive circles of the town. At such a moment, Bethel shows no inclination to resign her position to the weaklings around her. When Polly invokes *Cinderella* as the story of *her* own life ("'stepmother insurance'") Bethel's calculated reaction of self-pity is revealing. To her mind, the essential reality behind *Cinderella* is not the rise (so like her own) from the kitchen hearth to the kingdom, but rather the raw competition between the stepmother's family and Cinderella. Polly obviously believes in *Cinderella*, hoping that someday a glass slipper (!) will make escape a possibility for both Kenneth and herself. Unfortunately, George Sloan (no Prince Charming) proves himself all too susceptible to the sterile power of Bethel.

George and Bethel together, parody the loving, educational scenes with Polly and Kenneth. The inversion is completed when George *loses* his identity in succumbing to Bethel's proposal of marriage, while Kenneth *establishes* his conscious identity in proposing marriage to Polly, a proposal that is refused. Quite in keeping with the dark side of Reaney's humor is the devastating speed with which Bethel is able to force submerged hatred into the open:

I detested my father, he begat me after a stirring book on Gothic verb
tenses in a cold library . . .
. . . (and — mother?) . . .
She'd never wait till I could start my meal. She'd
pitch in and feed it to me like a baby till I was
twelve. She just shovelled it into my mouth.

[Act II, Sc. ix]

Bethel also skillfully exploits George's childhood hatred of Kenneth, finally pummelling him over sexual role-playing. In a perversion of the entire idea of sexuality and fertility, she runs him down in the weird chicken-and-egg argument over "who has the baby first"? Men or women? As Bethel snares George in her arms of good and evil, she parallels the success of Charlotte Shade in crushing Stephen's brief revolt in *The Sun and the Moon*.

Conflicting impulses in the artistic personality of the author balance these manic qualities in *The Easter Egg*. So, the human face of "The Bethel Story" is met and reversed by the events centred upon her stepson. Bethel is female, aggressive, lowborn, witty, greedy; versus Kenneth, who is male, passive (his physical rebellion is feeble), apparently catatonic ("pretty knives, forks, and spoons"), born to wealth, and dreamily contemplative. With its champion, the obsessive clock counting down to dinner, "The Bethel Story" is a violent continuation of the play's previous history of suicide, lightning, a ghost. Perhaps Kenneth's own story is closer to the essence of *The Easter Egg*, however. Although Kenneth does not realize it, the day is charged with omens for his future, for on the day of the party his godmother Mrs. Fuller has died. As his guardian during childhood (fairy godmother?), Mrs. Fuller had prevented Bethel from having Kenneth committed. She also gave Kenneth the easter egg shortly after the death of his father as a talisman of innocence and hope. Thought of as a play in which the giver of the gift dies on the day that the gift (after long years of burial) is found, a new form opens out for *The Easter Egg*. Kenneth is the young prince kept ignorant and a serving boy in his own castle. The play then acts out the final wish of Mrs. Fuller. Beneath the absurd surface of *The Easter Egg* is the beating heart of a fairytale.

The scene (Four) in which Polly continues her lessons with Kenneth is quite the &pposite of "neat and tidy" writing. Tension grows with the impatience of Kenneth at his slowness and inability, in contrast with the healing generous nature of Polly, who is a little nervous about the late arrival of George. The serious quality of the scene apparent in the long lists of civilized objects is undercut by ironies. Granted, the long lists are vital in later Reaney works. Here, though, the reams of words indicate first the tragicomic disparity between the words Kenneth has "learned" and the lack of meaning that many hold for him. Etiquette is an awkward ordeal, the threshold a struggle, and his recovery seems impossibly far away. Even Polly realizes that something more extreme is needed to bring Kenneth up (as the imagery of the play suggests), out of the water:

> Most of those words you've no idea of their meaning, but we're sowing them in your mind anyhow . . .
>
> [Act I, Sc. iv]

Her efforts to give Kenneth control of his environment through language also have a curiously self-preoccupied air that verges on the short-sighted. As Polly tartly criticizes the posture and grace of others, she fails to notice that Kenneth has said something fascinating to the clock.

> "Little clock, I'll tell the clock-doctor to
> Come and put all your little wheels asleep."
>
> [Act I, Sc. iv]

Kenneth is repeating the opening lines of *The Easter Egg*, containing Bethel's threat of euthanasia with regard to said clock (and Reaney wanted a real clock out in front of the curtain, going even during the intermission). The audience realizes, though Polly doesn't, that Kenneth has made a crucial connection between the future of the clock and his own question. If a mere clock may be physically threatened, what would Bethel force on a human who attempted to thwart her? A final ironic undertone to Kenneth's identification of the clock with himself is one the audience is left to ponder: are Polly's hands "too weak to wind *him* well"?

Another soul contested by the opposing forces of Polly and Bethel belongs (on the surface) to George Sloan, a diseased specimen of false maturity. By turns, George can be mischievous and weak (Scene Seven with Kenneth), decent if confused (Scene Eight with Polly), and finally sick and sadistic (Scene Nine with Bethel). As a character, George allows Reaney to focus the drift of *The Easter Egg* into moral chaos on the collapse of one individual. George is superficially much more adult than Kenneth, but as indicated in his lengthy courtship of Polly, the maturity masks a fundamental uncertainty. Despite this exchange with Bethel early in the hunt:

> (Polly would) . . . say it didn't matter. That evil is accidental, love is permanent.
> *Bethel*: Cheerful old Polly.
> *George*: What do you say?
> *Bethel*: I say good and evil's like two hands, mister . . . One left. One right. Both last forever.
>
> [Act II, Sc. ix]

George is unable to integrate his childhood fantasies into a stable personality. In an instructive contrast, Kenneth stops the toy train as it bears down on Anna Karenina, an action morally different from the more usual childish dreams of colossal toy train wrecks. George also provides a moral and psychological balance to Ira, who changes sides during the play, becoming more poetic and loving as George dissolves into an aspect of Bethel. Ira offers to make love with Bethel if she will allow Kenneth to come to him, while Bethel uses Kenneth as a foil in her assault on George. Again, there is a sharp contrast: for Ira, self-sacrifice ("throwing oneself"); for George, obsession and inertia. On both moral scales, the childlike and adult George — despite some good jokes — is a failure. If *The Easter Egg* were only "The Bethel Story," George Sloan might almost be the anti-hero: self-disgusted, repressed, and a cynical opportunist. Instead, he plays the role of depraved child/pathological villain. Twice there are curious scenes demonstrating the strength and awareness of his opponents. On both occasions, Kenneth and Ira — the true heroes — exhibit a common force able to dispose quickly of the supposed "normality" of George's rationalizations.

George lacks similar force and weight as a character because his preoccupations with decorum are at base irrelevant to the true movement of *The Easter Egg*. Ira (who also prophesies Bethel's eventual downfall) identifies this movement with the recovery of innocence imminent in Kenneth:

I looked up to see what my brother saw:
It was you. At five years old. Start naked.
Out of a silk scarf of your mother's you'd
made a turban. That was all your dress . . . A naked child
with all green light and sun streams about you.
You turned and vanished. I'll take that.
So far as I see that's what it all means.
And that naked innocent who gave me God
Is still lost in the forest and I shall bring him
Back to powerful friends who love him.

[Act I, Sc. ii]

The upheaval caused by Kenneth's metaphorical return resonates throughout the third act. Kenneth suddenly breaks through the window, abruptly rising from the pool where had been a young man asleep in a mirror, someone lost in the deluge, even a carp. At this moment two interpretations (at least) of the play's flow are possible. One holds that Bethel has repressed Kenneth, prevented him from maturing and marrying, in order to maintain her position as head of the house under the terms of the will left by Kenneth's father. Bethel schemed her way down the mountain into the heart of the village and has kept scheming ever since. The will proves why she did this. More consistent with the mood of the last scene however, is the notion of the strategic reappearance of the will as a parody of realistic motivation. A second interpretation would hold that what is surely paramount in this act is that Kenneth does break out. The blinding flash and magical sound when Kenneth again sees the egg announce the (re)birth of his character:

No, she's wrong, she's wrong. I had to have something if I was going to keep my head above water. No father, there was the kitten; no kitten, there was *this*. No this, there was immediately a skin over everything. Bethel's skin. When Polly gave me back this, this (*He walks about holding the egg above his head*) it was like being circumcised of a tight fold of skin that held you back from ever quite touching anything or being a father or seeing . . . it hurt like a rabbi with a sharp bright silver knife, it cut away Bethel's skin over my eyes and I saw.

[Act III, Sc. xii]

Kenneth becomes secure enough in his renewed identity to be anything he wishes, even macabre. The last words spoken by his father ("abyssal nothingness'') become part of the parlor game Kenneth plays with the others, part of his new control over his universe. The climax of *The Easter Egg* is reached at the moment Kenneth climbs out the parlor window, back into the evil past, able at last to free the little ghost girl. By this act of kindness, Kenneth asserts his benificent power over the bounds of his kingdom, and cleanses his father's house of blood.

The final moments of the play are packed with enormous tension. These opposing impulses accelerate and pull Kenneth and the pattern of action back and forth. One way lies back into the world of real time, and the impending party which will symbolize the apogee of the Bethel story. The other tendency pits the love of Polly and Ira against the terror of Bethel and the subservience of George.

Interestingly, Reaney avoids a clear cut resolution. As the play ends with Kenneth crossing the threshold, ready to greet Bethel's guests, there is ambiguity. Bethel has accepted the truth of her teacup prophecy with (suspicious) ease, but the irony extends further. The clock counting the minutes with painful regularity, presumably in fear of its life, mockingly strikes the half-hour. In the strange and wonderful universe of *The Easter Egg* even a clock may have its revenge, and its due.

The influence of *The Easter Egg* upon subsequent Reaney works is considerable. After this play, there are no more set changes, even when the action would seem to demand a change. Reaney discovered with *The Easter Egg* that the huge scope necessary in the romance conception of his theatre could be communicated as effectively in a front parlor as through the abrupt shifts of locale in *The Killdeer*, and *The Sun and the Moon*. The elastic geography of the house (a horror film convention) which allows the characters to bump into each other at random becomes an essential aspect of a theatre continually attempting to bring one manorhouse, or one county, to life in one dark room.

With its internal eccentricities and conflict, *The Easter Egg* remains the Reaney work furthest from the conventional stage. Perhaps the solution to the reverberating imbalances of Bethel versus Polly versus George versus Kenneth versus Ira is to play against the action and simply let the images ''float up.'' Perhaps the actors could start off with scripts in their hands and proceed. Life coming into the play, and going out, all the furious activity seen through a window.

Notes To Chapter Five

1. Reaney, James. ''Preface'' from *Masks of Childhood*, edited by Brian Parker, (Toronto, new press: 1972), p. vi.
2. Reaney, James. ''The Novels of Ivy Compton-Burnett,'' M.A. thesis, (University of Toronto, 1949), p. 1.
3. Reaney, James. *The Easter Egg* from *Masks of Childhood*, edited by Brian Parker, (Toronto: new press, 1972). Unless otherwise noted, all references are drawn from this edition.

6

The Sun and the Moon

Of the plays set explicitly in Perth County, *The Sun and the Moon*[1] is the most fully realized as an evocation of this entire society. In this work Reaney has given an attention to surface detail that is unlike the intense closeups of *The Killdeer* or the muted "reality" of *Listen to the Wind* or the mime of *Names and Nicknames*. The ambitious recreation of the Millbank milieu features accurate renderings of local dialect ("the saft," "wilted about this idea of mine"); preoccupations (many of my own relatives are still busy thinking up new Bible games); the fascination/repulsion with the "shacks across the river"; and especially institutions. Piano lessons, Young Peoples groups, croquet, and especially the Women's Institute meeting are all surveyed satirically and affectionately.

A useful comparison may be made with Stephen Leacock's satirical masterpiece *Sunshine Sketches of a Little Town*. Both authors face the same problem; that of reflecting the town accurately and universally without expressing only the alienation from its values that their big-city education implies. Critics have accused Leacock of being cold-hearted and condescending toward the Mariposans; I don't think this is entirely true because of his use of two conventions. The first convention is the adoption of a *persona* for narrative voice, at once an exact indication of the Mariposan state of mind, and a knowing wink at it. Leacock's second method of adjusting the Mariposan perspective is more complex and rewarding. European epic similes flow through the *Sunshine Sketches of a Little Town* connecting everyday life (Peter Pupkin) with grand and remote heroes (Tancred the Inconsolable). Mock-epic similes allow Leacock to keep Mariposa at the miniature and amusing level he wishes, while simultaneously making it valuable and worth conserving.

With Reaney and Millbank the problems are confronted somewhat differently. Rather than adopt a mock-epic frame of reference—though the constant Biblical epithets do supply ironic/mythic comparisons — Reaney makes the form of the play a tribute to Millbank. At the core of *The Sun and the Moon* is a kind of church basement theatre, using melodramatic devices and social realism to warn the faithful of the dangers of accepting a servant of the Archfiend as an apostle. For this reason the play also resembles an allegory credited with being a major childhood influence, *Satan or Christ? An Allegory Exposing the Soul-Destroying Vices of the Twentieth Century*. The allegory in this book may seem pretty bald, but the drama is undeniable as the most corpulent, smirking villain imaginable sets about trapping souls at amusement parks, church socials, anywhere . . . still losing every round to the servants of the Lord.

Reaney affirms the strength of Millbank, despite his skepticism. *The Sun and the Moon* is, in this way, a celebration of the milieu that remains a comfort and inspiration to the author. There are values in mythical Souwesto that reappear throughout the course of Reaney's theatre with a regularity matched by the different denunciations of Toronto (the mythic Babylon for Millbank):

> . . . next we're in Toronto on the top floor of the King George Hotel — and the bathroom has running cold and hot water — and, and — just for the heck of it I walk over and flush the real honest-to-goodness flush toilet just to see that such a thing could be.
>
> [p. 96]

Despite this affectionate irony, *The Sun and the Moon* does not strike us as a typical weekend in Millbank, even at the Kingbird's. The contrivance of the plot makes the base of *The Sun and the Moon* a parody/tribute to *The Scarlet Letter*:[2] the sin of a beloved minister unveiled not through the triumph of a personal struggle, but by accident. Although the revelation of Kingbird's affair with Mrs. Fall, and the climactic appearance of their "illegitimate" son, Frank, rock Millbank to its foundations, there is a sense of symmetry and design to this exposé . . . almost as if Kingbird had planned the shock, as a test of his flock:

> (Conybeare) Why not get the police constable?
> (Kingbird)   That would spoil it Felix. Too fussy. No — let's let it all ripen.
>
> [p. 129]

Even assuming that Kingbird is in control at this moment (unlikely), he can hardly have anticipated the cosmic disorder in Millbank. As the sun and the moon look across at each other for the first time in one hundred years, the male/female struggle indicated in the title breaks out. For Reaney, this is explained not so much in terms of social role-playing as in the acceptance of a certain beneficial order in both nature and civilization. So, the motion of *The Sun and the Moon* starts with Mrs. Fall's wish, years earlier:

> . . . My dreams had come true. Without marrying,
> Without falling in love I would have a child.

I would exist in male and female worlds
At one and the same time!

[p. 160]

What is wrong here is not to abandon the kitchen world for an independent
career, but to attempt to dominate both worlds at once. Edna Moody makes the
same mistake. She is unable to accept Kingbird as her minister; her efforts to
establish a tribal matriarchy through her office in the Women's Institute are
destructive, and her thoughtless support for Charlotte Shade nearly ends with
the disappearance of Andrew Kingbird into Shade's world. In keeping with
Reaney's drama, the characters are not particularly masculine or feminine.
Susan Kingbird is at ease in the supposedly "masculine" world of medical
research, while Felix Conybeare, Kingbird's fellow minister, is spinsterish
enough to be called down as a "shuddering male virgin." During the crisis all
familiar roles are brought into question, with the young people in the play
(Ralph and Susan, Frank and Ellen, Dennis and Stephen and Andrew) the most
disturbed by their inability to adapt to a microcosm in confusion.

In her efforts to displace Kingbird, Charlotte Shade incarnates the sexual
confusion that dislocates everyday life in Millbank. She skillfully compounds
an alarming variety of familiar male/female roles: abortionist (doctor); witch
(minister); sadist; housewife ('' . . . or this loaf/Will come prancing out of its
oven'') [p. 152]; mother/lover of Stephen; even medicine show:

. . . .with half a bottle of
Niagara Harmony Table Wine in
One hand and . . . oh *just inebriated*
That's the only word . . .

[p. 112]

Shade is finally characterized as subhuman, as her snuffling shortsightedness
apparently derives from the Nazgul, the Ringwraiths in *The Lord of the Rings*.
Her meaningless nomadism completes the construct of Shade as a total distor-
tion/inversion of Millbank, a phantasm symbolizing sterility and stasis.
Paradoxically, Millbank (settled, growing, civilized) finds Shade dangerously
attractive because "she doesn't even do what she wants to do." [p. 170]
Millbank's greatest reserve—its healthy distance from the glamorous Babylon
that is also "the bottom of all things''—is the quality that makes the village so
susceptible to Shade. Characters like Edna Moody are dissatisfied with their
position in this rural paradise, and their jealousy is the driving wheel in the plot
to supplant Kingbird. The vicious tramp sets Shade on Kingbird because he is
jealous of Kingbird's supposed complacency; Andrew is jealous of Susan and
Ralph for leaving behind their childhood together; Samuel Moody says of his
wife, "She wants to be you, Frank . . . she'd like/To get right up in the pulpit

and be you." [p. 117] Edna in her turn claims that Conybeare is jealous of her St. Charlotte, " . . . Jealous God doesn't show his power through you;" [p. 157] and Ruth Fall is finally able to round on Edna by laughing that Edna is jealous of her "sinful" past.

Under the influence of the evil that Shade tenders, this barely suppressed jealousy blossoms into withering hatred. Edna calls Frank Fall a monster without realizing she had nearly created a monstrous situation by refusing to allow Frank and her daughter, Ellen, a normal courtship. Ellen, in Toronto once before, had gone to Shade's house of dread . . . desperately considering an abortion. Samuel is correct in noting Edna's jealousy of Kingbird, too. Edna is so outraged at Francis Kingbird for marrying Ellen and Frank secretly, she champions Shade as his replacement (and victimized lover) without thinking. Shade herself says of the consequences:

> . . . Shame on you! You might have lost a very fine minister who I now declare I never laid eyes on before I came here Friday evening."
>
> [p. 165]

Vulnerable to Shade in darker, more mysterious ways are the adolescent young males in The *Sun and the Moon* who are lost in a miasma of sexual indeterminacy. Stephen ("stinking freemartin"), Dennis ("the whole rotting apparatus"), and Andrew ("her oldest girl should do") all exhibit an open hostility toward sexual relationships reflecting their own self-disgust and uncertainty.

Andrew, especially, typifies many of Reaney's flawed heroes. His private denunciation of his father ("you yourself whored after them thick and fast") [p. 130] is an explosion of destructive self-righteousness after the loss of an impossible innocence.

Ellen Fall, in contrast, publicly rejects Charlotte Shade:

> I took one look at her face—nasty shoddy smirking magician—and I ran away. And that's the woman you prefer to my Mr. Kingbird.
>
> [p. 165]

Ellen had been the first villager to choose Kingbird over Shade, and her denunciation of the "missionary" of evil encompasses the separate themes of *The Sun and the Moon* and binds them up. Frank and Ellen's child (who works in a chicken hatchery) is a sign of triumph over sexual confusion and repression, of fertility, and even social harmony as the baby will be grandchild to Reverend Kingbird, Ruth Fall, *and* the Moodys.

Andrew's reconciliation with his family and the discovery of the engagement ring brings *The Sun and the Moon* to a foreordained conclusion. Millbank has been choosing since the start of *The Sun and the Moon*: Kingbird or Shade? As the last to choose, Andrew makes the most meaningful decision. Beneath the self-consciously convoluted pattern of the play, the thrust of the action has been toward this final choice: will Andrew be able to accept the reunion of Ralph and Susan as married adults, and understand *his* father as the father of Frank Fall also? Andrew does return from Shade's camp. He is finally able to resist her directionless ''playfulness'' and painfully opens up to life in the new Millbank. He returns the lost engagement ring to Susan, and again accepts the world of his piano lessons, and of the boy with the bicycle or the man with the sack of grain — all metaphors of order and creation common to village life. Andrew's celebration of Ralph's and Susan's marriage completes the exile of Charlotte Shade, and the play ends with the image of Millbank fully transformed and healed.

Notes to Chapter Six

1. Reaney, James. *The Sun and the Moon* from *The Killdeer and Other Plays* (Toronto: Macmillan of Canada, 1962). Unless noted otherwise, all references are drawn from this edition.
2. Hawthorne, Nathaniel. *The Scarlet Letter*, (Boston: Ticknor, Read and Fields, 1850).

7

Three Desks

Three Desks[1] is the bittersweet paradox of James Reaney's comedies: at once
the funniest, most bitter, most personal, and perhaps least successful. Leaving
aside the question of its success (artistic, critical, and popular) for the time, an
examination of its other qualities reveals a close relation between humor,
atmosphere, and personality. As the funniest comedy, the play throws out
(throws away?) more jokes than any of the Perth County cycle, while, as the
most bitter, it is also the most terrifying and unresolved. As a personal work,
Three Desks is even more paradoxical. None of the Reaney constants (family,
community, mythic Souwesto) fortify the good characters; they are replaced
with the unusual—for his drama—factors of isolation, displacement, Rupertsland in the early fifties. Even though the main contestants may be equally
unusual characters (neurotic university professors instead of small towners and
farmers) the structure is similar to familiar elements in Reaney's work. The
claustrophobic nature of the office recalls the one-set universe of *The Easter
Egg*, collapsing the suggestion of infinity found in that play into some dreadful
human laboratory experiment. Also, in common with earlier works is the
ominous background of violent death. In *Three Desks*, the suicide of the
English department's previous junior lecturer compares with the deaths of the
Lorimers, or Ralph Ralph, as a warning to the characters who have survived.
What confirms this academic satire as Reaney's most personal work, however,
is not structure or ambience (the Winnipeg/Blue sequence in *Colours in the
Dark*, for instance). It is the intensity of autobiography when Edward Durelle,
arriving in the basement of the department offices eight minutes before his first
lecture, enters an environment that James Reaney entered under similar condi-
tions (of age, era). This does not equate Durelle with the author, of course, or
make the play a direct statement about Reaney's employment at the University
of Manitoba. But it is my belief that the strange, jarring mood of *Three Desks*
can best be explained as a reproduction of ten years in Manitoba. Therefore, as
the office, and then the whole college, becomes a battleground (where a whisper
is a gunshot), what is presented is not strictly documentary (''My Life, of a sort,
And Times, of a sort, with the English Dept''). *Three Desks* is a sensational,

unhappy satire using a modern commonplace (the office) as one corner of hell on earth.

Tension is derived from the location of this satire which, after all, must be rooted in some measure of reality in an utterly alien geography. So, the realism of the university milieu (squash, student caricatures, the foolish/great courses, paternalistic administration, even the absurd desk-pushing) is framed by the fierce horizon of an Arctic desert. The barren landscape, dominated by the heating plant, the icy river that offers no life or escape, and the wild extremes of heat and cold are all aspects of a mental universe, forming the background/interior of the characters. Reaney introduces the tension in the school song, which places a male chorus and a female chorus (a sexual polarity, as in the chess game later) under the baleful influence of a distant northern star. As the movement of the play proceeds to forty below (the heart of winter), the mood of the song may be increasingly seen as the mood of the play. Behind the jaunty, earnest lyrics ('' . . . Resolved that I should be a man and learn to drink some beer . . . Resolved that I should learn to cook and also read a book'') [Act I, Sc. i] lurks the despair of *Three Desks*. Concealed despair is, in fact, the structural metaphor provided first in the Rupertsland song. From the opening chorus, the innocuous college surface is exposed, revealing its arctic interior. A similar intensity is painfully disguised throughout *Three Desks*: mischievous desk-pushing is actually an assertion of territorial imperative; finally, murder. The characters explore the terrors of the ordinary and then discover their own capacity for childish ''little evils.'' Kilts, chess pieces, examinations, lexicons, paperknives are all ordinary weapons in this comedy of office guerrilla warfare.

Within this harsh, difficult environment are a group of characters all in some way stunted, and almost all qualifying as minor heroes. Sandy McWhin, the token Canadian is most obviously caricature, but still achieves a certain insane nobility by his mad Scottish ancestor worship. His status is reduced by his subservience to Niles and his cruelty to Mia. Edward Durelle, the nominal hero, is a mixture of Harry Gardner and George Sloan, cruel to Mia also, and weak enough to allow the ''happy ending'' to bury itself in Act One:

> I like you. I don't know why I do anything anymore. Like, why do we have colleges? Or read? Why do we think? What's the sense of it? Last year I began to feel all mixed up. It's the reason I lost my fellowship at Toronto, I just couldn't —
>
> [Act I, Sc. ii]

Durelle is capable of nervous charm (as balance) when he is courting Mia in topsy-turvy fashion, or mixing his gin with Winnie-the-Pooh. He is finally stunted by his adolescence (''like why'') his ''upside-down'' position, and is fortunate that Waterman and Mia are able to save him from Niles.

Mia Dubrovnic is the nominal heroine, and is placed deliberately in the play's water imagery:

> (*putting her hand under the tap*) This water is icy cold. It comes all the way from Raven Lake. (*She bathes her forehead.*)
>
> [Act I, Sc. iii]

In her case, water signifies her own cool, brilliant reserve (she *is* the provincial chess champion), and her (charismatic) ability to sweep the students into Homer. (Water imagery is healing, contemplative as an aspect of Waterman, while it makes of Niles a ''shark.'') Mia's underlying vulnerability—her collapse after the fight with Edward — is foreshadowed by her loveless, necessary affair with McWhin:

> I don't see very much in him, but whatever it is, it's enough. It might be called—the hangnail relationship or the tooth that's very nearly out. But he keeps touching some string in me—that I can't seem to keep him from touching.
>
> [Act I, Sc. iii]

A more comical, undergraduate counterpoint (nervous breakdowns, European family names) to the uncertain Edward and Mia romance is found in the Tuckersmith and Harcourt subplot. They alone, of the students, break free from Niles' influence, and only because they are helped by Waterman's fatherly good nature. Both Irwin and Deborah are lucky enough to escape from the play during the Christmas holidays.

At this point it does become necessary to discuss Maximilian Niles himself. Is Flossy Sorrin correct in forging ahead for her fifty per cent on the examination?

> I think the — I think that the real hero is Niles. Durelle's too weak; Waterman too fat. Look at Niles—young, powerful, mischievous. Is it his fault that no one can control him? This is very cleverly managed because we never see him alone *with* us; he's always the villain *apparently*. From down under, see . . .
>
> [Act II, Sc. viii]

Well, I have tried to mark this answer fairly, and it is admirably direct, but simply wrong-headed. A more reasonable view of Niles-as-hero is that he is heroic only to students such as Sorrin, (perhaps) himself (and perhaps the actor playing Niles, which might explain some of the reasons for defusing the role with Sorrin's statement). His energy is satanic, ultimately sadistic. Niles knows the secrets of others, and this knowledge is the source of his power. McWhin and Waterman (apparently) are both controlled by the threat of exposure. Those who are not unsuccessfully hiding their secret are still vulnerable to direct hits. Sorrin is overwhelmed by cynical charisma, and Mia is penetrated by dazzling psychoanalysis. In the final scene, as "The Principal Elect," Niles has apparently triumphed so completely that he has written his own ending to the play . . . Max to the principal's office! Jacob, appropriately humiliated by one last glimpse of the desks as they were before Niles; into enforced retirement! Edward Durelle dismissed! Mia to . . . the side of Max (if it still matters!) McWhin to the Residence! Then, just as . . . Checkmate! Niles (or as the stage directions (!) suggest "Hitler at Compiègne") is murdered by the true hero of *Three Desks*, Dr. Jacob Waterman.

Waterman is a Noah, a Hero in addition to his generous, decent qualities. He is connected with fertility ("rather a large family"); [Act I, Sc. i] order (Kings and Queens of England); knowledge preserved through the Great Darkness (his last lecture is to be on the Venerable Bede); and personal strength and self-sacrifice (King Arthur, Beowulf). Thrust close to the modern day surface of *Three Desks* is a heroic myth, narrating the epic conflict between a civilization in decline, and a rising force of superstitious, evil ignorance. As mythic figures, Waterman is King Arthur, and Niles (the "panther" with the "harem") is the chieftain of the Saxon hordes. Yet the final confrontation (offstage in a dusty, abandoned office) is hardly epic. Waterman kills Niles, more as one might kill a snake than a dragon, without mercy, and the play ends moments later. Again, a slight surface hides a complex interior.

To preserve his son's future, Waterman had once overmarked an examination that his son ought to have failed. Niles has the paper locked in his desk and torments Waterman with oblique references to this dark secret. Waterman retrieved the paper for a moment, only to see Niles smugly whisk it back into his prison-like desk. Still, this is not exactly what "causes" Waterman to murder.[2] Instead, when Niles tampers with the vanished past by rearranging the office, he unexpectedly rouses Waterman to cold fury. An idyllic memory (his desk in the sunlight) has been transformed into a hideous parody of its original state. Such memories, even illusions, are deeply necessary and give back humanity to a hellish earth. Waterman sees his tiny, golden universe mocked and strikes out. So the play ends with both triumph (death of Niles, rescue of the examination paper) and futility, as the last lines are also the opening lines of a court room trial. Even after wrestling with a demon, not an angel, Jacob is still too strong to collapse and thus fall out of his story. His very strength constricts him. Ironically, Jacob can't quite die a hero's death.

A further affirmation of Waterman as hero also confirms *Three Desks* as bearing the most personal signature. Education is a privileged, even magical process in other Reaney plays. Here, Waterman is its besieged guardian. The brief reading from Beowulf — as Jacob and Edward simply transcend the electronic buzzings — offers a fragment of the ideal universe. Waterman embodies the hope for such a future, and presently nourishes and protects the good, the true, the just. Combined with the autobiographical intensity already mentioned, this personification of the ideal makes *Three Desks* a violent, contradictory work. Nowhere else does Reaney place his characters and themes in so barren yet essential an arena.

Personal signature or no, *Three Desks* has not been well received. Considerable hostility has been directed at the primitive/shock-corridor effects (Mia's collapse after the chess game, the directly symbolic descriptions of the office). Other criticisms have attacked the play for being too melodramatic (the killing) *or* too realistic (the setting and language). Reaney himself appears dissatisfied with the result, and may write another academic comedy.[3]

Although I applaud the decision to kill the devil as a finish to the play, *Three Desks* is (for me) Reaney's least enjoyable drama. Scenes and moods crash into language and action with a pattern inherent in their collision alone. Reaney's usual method lies in the opposite direction. Form has emerged from (seemingly) chaotic and disassociated material. *Three Desks* is washed in private emotion, and its form never emerges properly.

Despite my complaints about lack of form, there are suggestions of careful visual design, more common in cinema than theatre. The collision of dynamics (choir, language, chess) is complemented by a consistent sense of visual form. Several scenes fade out on characters holding pieces of paper (even the Sheldonian types may be applicable) preparing for the time when Waterman will hold up the soul of his son.

Despite its controversial nature, *Three Desks* may therefore find its true form. Suitably distanced by the camera, there is the possibility of discovering the bureaucratic closeup comedy that resides in the material.

Notes to Chapter Seven

1. Reaney, James. *Three Desks* from *Masks of Childhood*, edited by Brian Parker, (Toronto: new press, 1972). Unless noted otherwise, all references are drawn from this edition.
2. There is a suggestion here of the drama in the closing scene of *The Sun and the Moon*: would Kingbird have killed Charlotte Shade to save Andrew?
3. *Three Desks* steps out to include an homage to one of the great satires of university life, *Lucky Jim* by Kingsley Amis. When Mr. Niles picks up the phone with the remark, "This is English, Professor Niles speaking" he is echoing an idiot somewhere in Amis' novel.

8

Colours in the Dark

Colours in the Dark[1] is drawn out of a "play box," a collection of possessions and treasures given archetypal order and coherence. The playbox and its objects create the play as each property is contemplated, remembered, and placed with a personal and epic design. Reaney calls this pattern "the back bone of a person growing up" [p. 5] although this feeling of autobiography hardly prepares one for the play's range of growing up experiences.

An analogy may be found in the reading of the Tarot card system. The imagery of *Colours in the Dark* is only occasionally indebted to the Tarot, but if one thinks of each unit in the play as a Tarot card, moving and falling into place on the table, one may grasp the form of the initially random associations. The Tarot, if read properly, should form a sentence both personally instructive and universally significant.

Colours in the Dark also clarifies itself as sentence/sequence as an attempt to describe personal, national, universal and moral history all at once. One recalls a work of similar purpose, Edmund Spenser's *The Faerie Queene*. Spenser's gigantic conception placed the hopes of the True Church and the British nation in the day-to-day life of the redeemed Christian. The ambition of Spenser's work is not duplicated in the play, which is a true Reaney omnibus relocating works from various stages throughout his artistic career in a less majestic (polemical) framework. *Colours in the Dark* narrates the stories of the Bible: of Canada; a biography (or autobiography) and archetypes of innocence, growth, and experience. The four stories are complementary, and ultimately the same story: so, Bible Sal announces her successfully completed recopy of the Book of Genesis immediately after the birth of the hero.

The personal and the cosmic are continually observed together. Bible Sal intervenes to note our progress through the Good Book, and the hero's environment advances from public school beating (an actual case involving my grandfather); to alienation as a university student; to utter disconnection as a university professor. The changes involved indicate that we are also watching Canada proceed as uncertainly as our hero through the present century. Canadian regions and cities are the setting and Canadian historical figures appear in a variety of guises. One might expect the play to be an impersonal and detached construction, using all of these elements with reserve and deliberation. Instead, *Colours in the Dark* is as deeply personal as is the "play box," allowing each private treasure to resonate with personal association. And what a range of personal association there is! The play that dreams itself out of the playbox celebrates anything from the Goderich primitive sculptor Laithwaite to the Disney *Snow White* (with the author speaking directly through Mr. Winemeyer):

> That's the only film I've ever seen and the only one I'll ever see. You can't go any higher than that in film art.
>
> [Act II, Sc. iv]

to several stories that assume the status of fables; to numerous and pointed Biblical references; to various kinds of poetry; to the 'thirties nostalgia of the *Little Orphan Annie* theme (consider the prevalence of orphans and courageous children in other Reaney plays); to material from other Reaney plays. The concerns are personal in origin, but epic in scope.

A great deal of the imagery of *Colours in the Dark* may be found in a 1959 poem "The Yellow Bellied Sapsucker" which contains not only a larger version of the existence poem (which in turn reappears in 1965 as "Gifts" in the form it takes in *Colours in the Dark*) as well as such figures as the tramp with the two canes (the dwarf/centaur in *The Sun and the Moon*, a whore on Yonge Street, even Shakespeare "with his no-handed Lavinia") which shows the tendency to personalize even the most famous and commonplace inspirations. This poem runs ninety lines and concludes (after middle stanzas of doubt and confusion):

> Golden Feather
> Of the yellow bellied sapsucker
> You are a golden spring
> A golden voice
> A golden tree and a golden torch
> By whose light and in whose world
> I show all complexity unfurled.[2]

Colours offers the same profusion of reference and experience as this poem but proceeds in a considerably different manner: instead of spelling out the fact that "God lies even in our excrement/what Bible says, a groundhog babbles too ... "[3] we sense this determination to find infinity in a grain of sand (Blake). The commonplace (the feather, the tramp, the whore and so on) are transformed into something of transcendent value in the strongest scenes of this play. It was noted that *Colours in the Dark* is not a mathematical concept, and as a rule number fifteen in Act One will not correspond directly to number fifteen in Act Two. There is at least one outstanding exception to this general rule. Unit Sixteen in the second act is the "Fable of the Baby and the Babysitter" which climaxes the play with the hero declaring his love for the cripple in these terms:

> Yes. I love you. Without your feet you walk with your breath. Without hands your body is a giant's hand. I love you."
>
> [Act I, Sc. xvi]

which recalls the information by Gramp and Gram back in Unit Sixteen of the first act:

> *Gramp*: Put your hands over your ears you can hear your feet walking beneath you. Crunch — Crunch.
> *Gram*: Put your hands over your feet—you can feel your breath walking — one breath in, one breath out.
>
> [Act I, Sc. xvi]

Otherwise the play is organized to illustrate the multiplicity of life: actors taking numerous roles (an idea developed even further in the Donnelly plays), constant recurrence of material (as in other lines of II, 16), the development of the existence poem; to return to the Tarot idea at the start, the realization that the same cards arise over and over again in startlingly different circumstances.

The organization is divided according to days of the week. According to colors: from the presence of all (white); through the rainbow; to the absence of all (black). According to the alphabet (the basic element of language: speech: which is the primal form of human civilization in the empty universe). It is also divided according to the elements of our solar system visible to the naked eye (starting with the sun and continuing to Jupiter and ending with the Earth), as well as according to various plants, both domestic and wild: in short, the way we choose to order time, society, space, gardens (elemental civilization) (Eden). In addition, some songs are invoked by the colors from the hobo's hymn "The Big Rock Candy Mountain" (in the white Eden birth sequence with images of paradisal "cigarette trees") to the "Japanese Sandman" (popular music in the twenties) to the hymns of the Sharon Temple builder David Wilson (an attempt to rebuild the perfect society (Eden) in the fallen world of Southern Ontario). The plants have their pattern too: the trillium (also the provincial flower of Ontario where so much of the action takes place); the orange lily (surely early July); Indian pipes (a fungus). The date of the purple unit is given as Hallowe'en, leaving the play on the edge of winter. Seven days: colors: planets: letters: groupings: constitute a re-ordering of the seven stars: candlesticks: angels: lamps: seals: plagues: kings of the Book of Revelations.

The number seven becomes a source of mystery and power as it operates throughout *Colours in the Dark*. Granny Crack has seven petticoats. Snow White is helped by seven dwarfs. Fragments of the existence poem appear on seven different occasions. Death carries seven people into His Kingdom, only to be defeated in a battle that takes seven turns of fortune. Above the concealed pattern of the sevens is the obvious family pyramid of

$$2::4::8::16::32::64::128::256::512::1024$$

ancestors, soulmakers, growing up experiences. These numbers are spoken by the whole chorus and attain a force comparable to the evolving nature of the existence poem: all these numbers make up the world for one child.

Thus, the structure of *Colours* is numerological and repetitive although the Black unit, Some Day, implies a revelation that will end the day to day :: letter to letter repetition. As an organizational principle this system allows Reaney a real freedom in the selection of material, inside the general contour of the movement from sickness to health. Discussing the component units themselves involves a certain prejudice of choice: for myself, the preferred scenes are those set in Souwesto. With some exceptions, I think the city units suffer from an extreme hostility, that is quite unlike the complex attitude Reaney is able to adopt in his treatment of the Souwesto material. Anyway, here are some of the individual units and sequences that seem pre-eminent to me.

Act One is set in the innocent world of Perth County, and the key enemy of this innocence is the Grizzly Bear. The bear symbolizes all the childhood fears of the great impersonal universe, even the darkness of the womb. In the "Little Red Riding Hood" takeoff of 8: "Berry Picking" the child first escapes the bear:

Sadie: (from inside the bear) . . .
            And still — I got eat up by a bear.
            Mother! Father! Chase the bear away!
MOTHER and FATHER in huge Mother-and-Father carnival heads come on like marionettes. Father slices the bear open. Out springs the devoured child. Mother sews the bear up.
Sadie: Oh — thank you Father and Mother — for giving me life.
                                                            [Act I, Sc. ix]

This scene recalls the birth-of-the-universe/birth-of-the-human scene in Act One Unit 4:

Pa: How can I be born? Who is stopping my sun from rising?
Gramp: (as a bear) I am. I'm Grizzly Bear and I've crossed your mother's
            legs and you'll never see the earth get up or the light come down.
Pa: Blind as I am, Sundogs — I've heard you barking on either side

of me—sick the bear away where he's got his paw over the Sun.
Make him let go of my arm!
The Sundogs chase away the bear. All the kids come yapping across the
stage as dogs. Thunder! A bright light now fills the stage.

[Act I, Sc. iv]

The child and the bear scene is simplistic in its evocation of the child's idea of
birth, while the earlier scene is poetic in its impression of both sexual union,
and birth from the womb (cf., *One-man Masque* for Reaney's concept of the
battles faced in the womb by the embryonic child). The white light is several
things at once: the moment of conception, the illumination as the soul is born
(imagination), and the emergence into the blinding light of the world as the
child leaves the womb. For Little Red Riding Hood/Sadie the metaphorical sun
dogs are replaced by the actual mother and father who give the child life (escape
from the world of the womb) and then give the child a large portion of its
identity as it grows outward into the world and away from the fears and
self-centredness of the child. In saving the child from the bear, the mother and
father perform an operation (cutting and then sewing up again), and the bear
scrambles off with a pail of berries given by Sadie to feed its cubs. This
child-like explanation of the phenomenon of birth and identity indicates the
questions Sadie is capable of asking herself. The mysteries of men and women,
problems of identity, confusions of experience are reserved for the second act.
Sadie knows that both her parents have something to do with her birth although
where she came from and how she arrived are still unknown to her. The scene in
which there is the greatest conflict between children and adults is number
eleven: ''The Schoolmaster and Tecumseh.'' As the child grows older and goes
out into the world the heroic parents who defeat the Bear are replaced by various
surrogate parents (teachers, other adults who exercise some authority over the
child, and sometimes in cruel moments, the parents themselves). It is clear in
this scene that the schoolmaster is a sadistic monster who deserves to be fully
punished for abusing his authority over the vulnerable children. Another clever
adult (the Lawyer) conspires to take advantage of the ignorance of the children
and thus allow the teacher to escape. Now, these two roles are taken in
performance by the father (schoolmaster) and the mother (lawyer), and this
suggests another child-like concept of the world. As the child leaves the secure
and coddled world of its first years, the universe appears as a giant courtroom
with the adults forming a malicious kangaroo court for the purpose of meting
out punishment to children as the mood takes them. The children suddenly gain
the upper hand (signalling the inevitable day when they do become more
powerful than their parents), and begin whipping them (as in *Applebutter*). Just
as this universal fantasy of all oppressed children is about to take its course,
Tecumseh appears and cries out: (played by Gramp)

Stop! These whips are made of my skin which the Yankees flayed from my back when I was killed long with a Kentuckyman's rifle at the battle of Moraviantown . . .

[Act I, Sc. xi]

The sudden transition from the fantastic and macabre world of the whippings to the mythic/historic character of Tecumseh changes the tone of the passage. We see the history of the whippings in a different perspective: Tecumseh, a great hero was once mutilated right in Souwesto following an actual battle for Canada. Tecumseh becomes the heroic nature-spirit who turns into a tortoise, explains his ancestry (''My mother was the moon, my father the sun'') [Act I, Sc. xi] and invokes the transition from the sun to the moon for the hero in units four and five. Tecumseh is able to carry the children on his back to meet their actual ancestors because he is part of their ancestry, part of their collective unconscious (one of the children identifies the time of Moraviantown). The epic catalogue of the names of the ships that brought our ancestors evokes the incredible diversity of Canadian civilization and brings us along historically from the War of 1812 through the nineteenth and early twentieth centuries. There are figures from Greek myth and history, birds, French, British and so forth. The Orange Parade and the scenes of religious baiting suggest what happened to most of these ancestors as they tried to adapt to Canada. The walking scene carries forward the childhood questions of origin and memories. The Ode on the Mammoth Cheese shows us that Souwesto always had its bards and that this one even wrote something about ''Night Blooming Cereus.'' The town is seen for the first time: a 1910 store confronts the mystery of life and death throughout the string scene. The concluding unit: magic square is the controversial ''The Bridge or Even Adolf Hitler had 1024 Great Great Great Great Great Great Great Great Grandparents and Kept a Play Box Too.'' Well, the time has come for the child to leave the world of innocence and become a well-adjusted adult: or as the Tarot cards put it, ''the upside down *Hangedman* (September) is the boy at puberty''[4] . . . Hitler is seen as the inverted child as in Antichrist who does not grow outward but retains his youthful mask of innocence even as the face behind it goes rotten with hatred and insanity. In short, a skull that looks forward to the death figures of the closing unit squares. The hero finds himself like ''one of those people you hear about in mental hospitals who can't go through a doorway.'' [Act I, Sc. xxi] The soul-building pyramid inverts to a Nazi rally and the cradled baby is revealed as Hitler: the shock effect is powerful and takes us into the lobby wondering.

The second act takes us through the world of experience as the hero wanders, like the lost tribes of Israel, in search of love and imagination carrying the piece of the star given to him by Mr. Winemeyer, the primitive artist and hermit (the tarot structure again) and the green leaf of love that Bible Sal has given him when they were fishing: "Adam and Eve could have hidden all their shame in it." [Act II, Sc. ix] There are three key sequences in the second act narrating the progress of the hero through the flux of the city into the marriage of number eighteen; these are the units with Winemeyer and the piano teacher (two through six), the confrontation with Professor Button (nine), and the aforementioned "The Fable of the Baby Sitter and the Baby."

In the Winemeyer sequences Reaney is able to blend and mix several local sources to great effect: Winemeyer, the eccentric old hermit who puzzled South Easthope farmers with his wizardly aura; some familiar primitive/sophisticated Souwesto culture; some typical jokes (as far as I know Laithwaite has no sculpture of "the infant Riel suckled by the buffalo Manitoba" [Act II, Sc. iv]; the oblique parable of the peacock and the jealous pig. A piano lesson connects the drawing room in town with the magic and wonder of Winemeyer's farm as the hero finds the piece of the star again after performing "The Cloud" so well. The question the hero poses as the music teacher calmly/transcendentally plays the same hymn as Winemeyer: "Miss Miller. Tell me the truth. Are you really Mr. Winemeyer in disguise? Are men and women really the same?" [Act II, Sc. v] is not the tortured moment of self-doubt and sexual confusion that Reaney's heroes so often undergo. Instead, the hero is still questioning as might a child, and remains a curious innocent. Mr. Winemeyer's death is a great shock. While he has been experimenting with reincarnation, a startling moment erupts when the hermit crawls into the magic log and emerges as the luna moth which flies to Sharon Temple: Winemeyer is an Old Testament prophet who can only preach to the tribe and point the way to the heaven on earth, he is not able to take the boy with him. The story Winemeyer tells about the peculiar kind of soup works along the same lines as the more serious Cain/Abel poem (the gift given by Abel is a piece of gravel). The first boy is still very much small town in his ways, earnest and genuinely shocked at the disclosure that his friend not only does not go to church but has slept with several women (at least!). The second boy is full of false sophistication and, as it turns out, is lying about his lapses in the city anyway. For all that the second boy pretends to know, it is indicative of his fall that he does ladle into the soup with gusto and without thinking. The circumstances of the visit are also strange: the two young men are visiting a married young woman they both like, but since she has just given birth, she won't be seen much, and they will be spending time with her husband, who they don't much like. After the dinner the first young man reveals that it was horse meat and soup that they were both offered and that Boy Two has eaten so heartily:

Boy 2:   Why didn't you tell me?
Boy 1:   That it was horse a soup? I thought you'd know since you'd gone away to law school and become so smart and had so much experience.

Boy 2: (mimes vomiting)
         Oh you fool. It was all a lie. Things like that are mostly lies. It
         was a lie.
Boy 1: (with Hermit and Boy 1 talking together)
         It's not a lie now, is it? It's not a lie now . . .

                                                          [Act II, Sc. iii]

Now, in reorganizing this scene we see the Hermit played by Gramp, telling
a story about his past and casting his son in the role of the false sophisticate and
his grandson as the outraged small-towner. As a father to the child the hero has a
secure sexual identity: through his marriage he has stabilized his sense of the
world by fathering children. The son is worried enough to ask Mr. Winemeyer
"Am I potentially homosexual?" [Act II, Sc. iii] at the start of the story, and his
character assumes the instability of the false sophisticate in different ways. The
false sophisticate has committed a crime or other (to use the accusation made
against the hero throughout), but it is not the sexual initiation he pretends to or
even his announced disbelief in hell that constitutes his crime. Rather it is this
remark:

   I didn't realize how sleepy life was here till I came back this Saturday. You
   can tell just by the sound of the minister's voice.

                                                          [Act II, Sc. iii]

What makes remarks like this a crime is that they amount to innocence being
criticized and dismissed by experience (and not too much experience at that) for
being "sleepy." As we have seen the world of innocence in the first act is by no
means sleepy, and when the false city dweller attempts to dismiss the life of the
town in these terms, he is only a fool. He is not using his experience to rebuild a
new world of redeemed innocence, but is only revealing the distortions his
innocence is undergoing. The son as Boy One (the youthful Mr. Winemeyer) is
sexually defensive and still equates the thought with the deed; because the story
is no lie to him, he is as cruel to his friend Jacob physically, as Jake has been
cruel mentally in dismissing the life of the town. The vomiting seems the
appropriate punishment to him for what Jake has said about things that mean so
much to Boy One. The final paradox is that the story is a memory of Mr.
Winemeyer who, as the hermit, should teach the hero prudence under the Tarot
system. In terms of the play it is not so much "prudent" as a suggestion of how
to regain your innocence in the world.

   Professor Button is the inversion of Mr. Winemeyer and Miss Miller: while
they have remained as prophetic figures in their neighborhood, Button has
gathered great knowledge and become a force of mystification in the university,
where so many of the young and confused find themselves trying to find
themselves. Button is extremely learned ("President of the Oriental Institute")

and uses this mostly to dismiss his students as precocious and to battle Kabuki-style with the idealistic, confused hero who is still maintaining that "A flower is like a star."

> Oachghwkwk! A flower is not like a star! Nothing is like anyone else. Anything else. You've got to get over thinking things are like other things.
>
> [Act II, Sc. ix]

This utter cynicism is a manifestation of the Grizzly Bear who has his paw over the sun of the hero and won't let his imaginative identity be born. Button is cynical about sexuality, his students, his fellow experts and even about Bible Sal, which is his downfall:

> Why there's a girl in our college kitchens who's not only copying out the whole Bible into Woolworth's scribblers, but believes literally every word it says.
>
> [Act II, Sc. ix]

Bible Sal accepts the battle of speaking in tongues with Button after some preliminary skirmishes over the verses of the Bible. The climax comes when she defeats him at his own specialty, Ancient Babylonian, (Under this empire he would be a lord and she an Israelite in captivity.)

> *Button*   Bresith bara elohim eth kassamayim weth haarec.
> *Sal*   Whaarec hayatha tho hu wabbobu whoselch appne thehim. Weruah marahepheth hammayim wayymen yehi or YEHI or WAYEHI WAYEHI
>
> [Act II, Sc. ix]

The defeat of Button makes possible the transition from simile (the flower is like a star) to metaphor (the flower is a star) and the state of love under whose influence the cohesion and identity of the universe seems finally to be taking place.

But for the hero the trials continue. Having lost both the green leaf of love and the starpiece, he is doomed to wander alone in search of identity and faith. Bible Sal is unable to convince the hero by herself, as he petulantly resists her embrace. She does find renewed inspiration in her victory over Button, which places the passage in its Biblical context. "But instead I'll finish copying out the whole Bible. Tonight — I'll begin with the New Testament. I have the strength at last to write of Jesus." [Act II, Sc. ix] The wanderings of the hero take him through Winnipeg and Toronto (units ten through fifteen) which conclude with his cursing of Prometheus for inventing fire and begetting technology.

Unit number sixteen, "The Fable of the Babysitter and the Baby," is one of the crucial scenes of *Colours in the Dark*. We have watched the hero contend with some of the evils of childhood and maturity, and cope with them adequately. In this scene he must come to terms with the disease and illness inherent in human reproduction, with the way some humans are born deformed and unable to cope by themselves: really with the existence of death in life. Faced with the monstrous "baby" who has been born without arms and legs, the hero at first reacts with horror:

> I have no love to spare. I can't bear sickness and pain in myself or others. I reject completely all the messy ways we sail coffins in our seed. Don't you curse your parents' lust?
>
> [Act II, Sc. xvi]

The statement recalls desperate rejection of Owen by Mrs. Taylor, "I can't stand sickness and death, You gave me two children who died."[5] Both statements indicate lack of maturity: an inability to accept life as it is, complete with ugly and unexplained disease. This weakness keeps the hero somehow blind (he cannot see because "he has his hands over his eyes"). When he does relent and begin to read from the Ranch Romances (love of the Universe in the most likely place) he finds the green leaf of love he had lost earlier. As the "baby" explains, "things you've lost are inside things you don't like." [Act II, Sc. xvi] The hero opens up himself, as he reluctantly opens the Ranch Romances, and finds that he *can* see. Existence has finally taught itself to the hero, and his act of love makes possible this revelation. He is now ready for marriage (green leaf) at the Sharon Temple (where the luna moth that was Mr. Winemeyer fluttered). Using the same odd time scheme as *Listen to the Wind* in which marriage is followed almost immediately by death, the scene changes, to the Dance of Death in London, Ontario. Various of the occupations rhymed off in Act I: Scene i are driven into the country of Death. After this enslavement, there is a sinister return to the childlike conception of battle with Death. The children win another victory in the form of a scissors/paper/stone type of game in which the sacrifice of the strong uncle saves the last baby left alive from the rat in the cage.

Unit 21 in the second act brings the action back to the party game of guessing colors in the dark, as if the play had lasted only an instant as the father explained (and thought to himself) how he had become adept at guessing the colors. The sick child, ill in his bed for forty days (the same duration as Jesus in the wilderness) is well again. His mother reports that the child nearly did die several times but has fully recovered, and it is springtime: "And the grass is green. The branches are covered with leaves." [Act II, Sc. xxi]

As the story ends with health and revelation, the conception of *Colours in the Dark* also finishes its ambitious design. Proposing to narrate the whole history of a life, the history of the world through the medium of the Bible, and to illustrate impersonal thoughts on life and death, Reaney has chosen to use a full range of dramatic devices of—"colours in the dark." There are slides, songs, fragments of the existence poem, dialogue, choral work: total multi-media semiology. The density of the story dictates manipulation of all this material for a single end, that of involving the spectator in the epic quest, in the battle with Death. Reducing many of the experiences to childlike conceptions allows a ready-made identification, and the constant repetition of questions, poetry, and characters strengthens the handhold through the labyrinth. As *Colours* ends with the family pyramid, the quest is completed, and the cycles have resolved their turning. We have passed through the labyrinth of life, sickness, death, winter, and the seven elements, and should have begun to identify this one child with ourselves.

Notes to Chapter Eight

1. Reaney, James. *Colours in the Dark*, edited by Peter Hay, (Vancouver: Talonbooks, 1971). Unless noted otherwise, all references are drawn from this edition.
2. Reaney, James. "The Yellow-Bellied Sapsucker" from *Poems*, edited by Germaine Warkentin, (Toronto: new press, 1972), p. 118.
3. Reaney, James. "The Yellow-Bellied Sapsucker" from *Poems*, edited by Germaine Warkentin, (Toronto: new press, 1972), p. 118.
4. Raine Kathleen. *Yeats, the Tarot and the Golden Dawn*, (Dublin: The Dolmen Press, 1972), p. 25.
5. Reaney, James. *Listen to the Wind*, (Vancouver: Talon books, 1972), Act III, Sc. xlv, xlvi and xlvii.

9

The Donnellys

If Souwesto is as Gothic as its churches and farms appear at twilight or before a summer storm, then the great work that defines this is *The Black Donnellys*[1] by Thomas Kelley. This stupendously successful account of the events preceding the murder of the Donnellys in 1880, this joyfully grim justification of those murders, has become one of the most widely-read works of Canadian fiction. I choose my words with caution at this point; while Kelley's tale has a certain pretense of authenticity, it should not be read as an objective or even as an accurate rendering of the facts concerning the Biddulph horror. *The Black Donnellys*, a tremendously enjoyable, wildly energetic, hopelessly clichéd thriller tells the Donnelly story after a fashion but does not tell much truth about the Donnellys. The work remains the most popular account of the family and their neighbors, and any subsequent adjustment of the tale must face public comparison with the Kelley version.

James Reaney, in his Donnelly trilogy (*Sticks and Stones, The Donnellys, Part One*,[2] then "The St. Nicholas Hotel," and finally "Handcuffs"), has taken a decidedly anti-Kelley position in his portrayal of the Donnellys, even lampooning Kelley's extreme characterizations with the stage directions:

> The False Donnelly actors should be the Grand Guignol persons of folklore — wild cats on hot stoves.
>
> [p. 23]

Nevertheless, his attitude to the Donnellys is considerably indebted to Kelley's efforts to paint the family as the worst of cutthroats and savages. Kelley was following the popular anti-Donnelly tradition in his book, after all, and if his Donnellys were too stupidly evil and destructive to be believed, it is only recently that the minority pro-Donnelly view has gained much circulation. The chief manifesto of the view that is more sympathetic to the Donnellys is Orlo Miller's *The Donnellys Must Die*,[3] an historical interpretation of the family feud that attempts to trace its origins to secret societies in Ireland. Reaney has written that it is this double point of view, the mystery inherent in the contrasting accounts presented by Kelley and Miller that first interested him in the potential of the Donnelly story for dramatic adaptation.[4] As his interest in the mystery of the family murdered by a mob of their neighbors increased, Reaney began to do his own research through old newspaper files, interviews, and court documents. The Donnellys in Reaney's trilogy, in fact, take several steps further than the family in Miller's book. These Donnellys are no longer simply a family that was much less black-hearted than previously thought; they are treated as rather noble, somewhat better than their neighbors and, generally, violent only after provocation. If there is a tension threatening to disrupt Reaney's trilogy, it is this portrait of the Donnellys as proud, strong, great. At times. In his efforts to correct the impression created by Kelley, Reaney abandons the ambiguity that drew him to the story in the first place and seems to be writing his own wild, energetic, clichéd popular thriller called the "White" Donnellys.

While Reaney exhibits impatience with other (more Kelley oriented) accounts of the Donnellys, he has also provided a system of balances to counter his own pro-Donnelly prejudices. He utilized the competition of two groups over something of value (in this case, the kind of life possible in the New World). He also used the epic structure with local history (as in the Norse *Saga of Njal*).[5] He felt a real empathy for the family as a unit. For the Donnellys, their family was the loyal and civilized structure in a malevolent and savage world, and the strength and beauty of the family relationships (this time there is no tyrant) among the Donnellys is one of Reaney's greatest achievements as a dramatist.

My own feeling is that it is still premature to comment on *The Donnellys*, in the same way that one may comment on the structure of *The Easter Egg*. *Sticks and Stones* has been published, but "The St. Nicholas Hotel" and "Hand-cuffs" have not. Rather than attempt a critique of the work published and unpublished, I will limit my discussion to the techniques adopted by Reaney in organizing this vast amount of material (there are eighty characters in "The St. Nicholas Hotel") and on the explanation he offers for the murders.

Orlo Miller, at one particularly knotted piece of argument, interrupts the flow of *The Donnellys Must Die* to apologize:

> At first glance the introduction of Charles Kent into the Biddulph feud seems a digression. The thing is dramatically untidy. He is like the red herring introduced unfairly by the amateur mystery story writer to confuse the reader. Here we have a respectable resident of a city sixteen miles away from the seat of warfare becoming accidentally involved in a quarrel not of his own making, nor indeed known to him.[6]

Reaney divides this contorted reality into four rituals of life in Biddulph: the seasonal, introduced by the drinking song "John Barleycorn," the story of the "dying god . . . who is killed at the height of his powers"[7]; the spiritual, present in the first line spoken in *Sticks and Stones*, ''Which are the sacraments that can be received only once?''; the legal and the geometric, evident in the surveying and census-taking that follows the story Mrs. Donnelly tells Will about his father's defiance of the Whitefeet in Ireland. These realities of life in the wild lands of Canada West are immutable. The surveyor who sets out the Donnelly's lot predicts that controversy will arise because of the little stream that runs through it, the laws of geometry not withstanding. While eternal forces in the Donnelly's life, these factors are by no means at peace with one another. The effort to force a legal geometric division of land on the territory causes the problems alluded to by the surveyor, and the rigorous attempt to establish a uniform law (implied by the recital of the details of court documents throughout the play) also fails. Donnelly and Cassleigh both kill men they hate, but the circumstances and treatment accorded by the law are so different that the crimes seem to exist in separate worlds. The legal may reach over and interfere with the seasonal: the Donnellys watch as half their crop is transferred to a new owner:

> That wheat is lost. And my scythe never touched it. . . . It was harvested by a piece of paper. I've known men burn their crop rather than have a stranger harvest it.
>
> [p. 20]

These are the codes of existence in Biddulph: they demand strict adherence, and are capable of betraying even the most devoted supplicant.

The Donnellys are inhabitants of the seasonal world of nature and fertility. The family is constantly seen harvesting, planting, clearing the land, bringing up their eight children, even dying into the soil. ''John Barleycorn'' is the natural process with which they are identified. The ballad has its pattern of ploughing, first shoots, growth, harvest, threshing, distilling, and, finally, drunkard's piss against the wall. The Donnellys' own story is something like this. A rich natural force is smashed down by the weight of society and pissed away. Excremental imagery of this sort dominates the verbal pattern of ''The St. Nicholas Hotel.'' The ballad fades into the body of the play, but the identification of the Donnellys with the barley is made explicit in several sections of the work. Mr. Donnelly often compares his sons to the seeds of young shoots that will rise up after he is gone. During the flashback to his defiance of the Whitefeet, there is a subliminal equation of Donnellys and wheat. The Whitefeet summon Donnelly to face them outside the door. Donnelly continues with a verse later in the episode:

Male Voice	Jim Donnelly!
Others	Then the binder came with her neat thumb; She bound me all around

Male Voice	Jim Donnelly!
Others	And then they hired a handyman To stand me to the ground
Male Voice	Jim Donnelly!

[p. 3]

Even before much is known about the Donnellys in Ireland or Biddulph, the impression of the natural pattern of their existence has been reinforced.

Next to the natural order of the Donnellys, there is the spiritual world of the Church, and in a clandestine sense, a kind of secret society. The form of the play involves the response of a Donnelly to a question established by tradition. It might be religious, as the cool demand of the priest:

Will, would you know then how to address the bishop with the proper form of his title if you should decide to ask him this question of yours?

[p. 17]

It might be the Donnellys, asking themselves something, trying to puzzle out the reasons for their constricted life: "Why is our father's farm so narrow?" [p. 20] It might be also a thinly veiled threat:

Did you not know, Jim Donnelly, that no Whitefoot is to have any dealings with the Protestant and the heretic Johnson?

[p. 4]

This last inquiry illustrates the demonic undercurrent of secret religion running through the base of the play. For each priest in the daylight, effective as a spiritual counsellor to his parishioners or not, there is a figure like Cassleigh with his inversion of the fifth commandment:

The fifth commandment of God is: Thou, Brimmacombe — should not have seen me beaten so badly. . . .

[p. 14]

When Mr. Donnelly refuses to swear allegiance to the Whitefeet and their mythical leader, Matthew Midnight, he also refuses membership in the secret church. Besides Cassleigh's new commandment, this church of the night is complete with vestments (the women's clothing they use as disguises), rituals (the barrel), invocations (the threats to visit Donnelly at some hour of the day or the night), and sacraments (the burning barns and houses of their enemies). Donnelly does not kneel in confirmation of this black mass, and yet the Donnelly's relations with their true priests are never as free and holy as they should be. In "The St. Nicholas Hotel" it is the parish priest who organizes the vigilante committee that eventually murders five of the family (this is a true fact). Thus, the Donnellys are separate from both spiritual worlds of Biddulph the true and the demonic. They may attend Mass with their fellow Irish settlers, but the Donnellys are never securely confirmed into the community or the church. The final force of the questioning lies in its allusion to the sacrament of Confirmation. Question after question (some textual parodies of the actual literature of Confirmation) constructs the form of the play. The Donnellys wait nervously as the Bishop tests the other parishioners around them, to find out if the name of The Donnellys may be added to the soldiers of Christ or respected citizens of Biddulph. At the finish of *Sticks and Stones*, the Donnellys have been rejected but resolve to stay on in the township: ''Donnellys don't kneel.''[p. 50]

The enemies of the family also use the legal power of deed and title and court procedure in their battle to force the Donnellys to kneel. One of their chief opponents is George Stub, a Protestant businessman, who rises to the position of magistrate through his Conservative political connections. Stub is the Donnellys' landlord, but this does not prevent him from treating them maliciously. It is Stub who gives Mrs. Donnelly dishonest *legal* advice about the chances of Mr. Donnelly escaping with a reduced charge after he has killed Farl at the logging bee. Stub taunts the young, crippled, romantic William Donnelly from the safety of his magistrate's chair. Mrs. Donnelly soon turns the tables on Stub, however, when she reminds the court of Stub's own story: from arsonist and rioter to magistrate.

The laws of geometry affect the whole horizon of Biddulph, and is the element of the play most difficult to describe. It is one thing to read about the roads which are at once neighbor's homes and enemy territory, and another to see the characters tangled with ladders, sticks and stones, and the unnatural forms of their farms. The wild new country seems to close into a small tight ''pound'' as Mrs. Donnelly calls it, instead of expanding into infinity. All the characters feel this right-angled confinement, and this congestion is partly the cause of the intensity with which the Donnellys are hated.

Under this shape of Biddulph, Reaney puts forward his explanation of the murder of the Donnellys. The reasons are social, historical, and psychological: the first two (the Donnelly's friendship with Protestants and their refusal to join the Whitefeet) are derived from *The Donnellys Must Die*, although less emphasis is placed on this cause in *Sticks and Stones* than in Miller's research.[8] The historical aspect of the feud is a consequence of Mr. Donnelly's escape from the sentence of death in the Farl killing. As Mrs. Donnelly walks to Goderich for justice, she adds signatures collected by the local MP to add to her own petition:

Hurrah for Holmes will be our cry from now on in. Our family's vote is Grit forever and I've seven sons who'll agree or else. . . .

[p. 34]

There is a tragic implication in the heroic and proud request for the commutation of her husband's sentence. Even as she walks to Goderich (in an *homage* to
Jeanie Dean's walk to London and Queen Caroline in *The Heart of Midlo-
thian*), Mrs. Donnelly sows the seeds of her destruction. As staunch Grits in a
predominantly Tory riding (and this before the days of the secret ballot), the
Donnellys are soon marked by Stub and the Conservative machine as dangerous
enemies. The fearless quality of the Donnellys gives them great reserves of
pride and dignity, but it also makes them unique. The seriousness of the
political issue is brought forward in the second play, "The St. Nicholas
Hotel." Here it is strongly suggested that the election of 1878 sealed their fate.
Their defiant Liberal voting outraged the London Tories much as their original
defiance of the Whitefeet had marked them as outcasts. Mr. Donnelly remarks
on this to Stub, after the Donnelly's barn has been burnt, a hint that they should
leave before any further action is taken:

> Gallagher has eight boys. Do you want to know, Mr. Stub, why we never
> hear you complaining of hordes of Gallaghers bursting this township at the
> seams? Because the Gallaghers vote Tory, the way you do now. And I
> guess it's only Grits who musn't multiply (*Pause*) like myself. . . .
>
> [p. 48]

The defiance is what marks the Donnellys as psychologically unique: it is the
source of their strength and (as implied earlier) the cause of their isolation. In a
county dominated by fear and half-hidden violence, the ability of the Donnellys
to stand alone and say:

> But you see I won't kneel. And I won't, I will not swear that.
>
> [p. 4]

frightens and enrages their enemies. This coherence of history (the feud) and
character (the individual defiance) is the reason that the Donnellys must die.
Reaney is able to develop the character of the Donnellys further than does Orlo
Miller, and his portrait of Mr. and Mrs. Donnelly in words and action shows
their strength together, and presents the foreboding of how that mutual strength
might someday prove a fatal weakness.

Mrs. Donnelly is the dominant figure in *Sticks and Stones*. Johannah or
Judith is a mother, a wife, and leader of the clan. Enemies of the Donnellys
have always attempted to deride her as a coarse giantess (and do so in "The St.
Nicholas Hotel"), but in *Sticks and Stones* she is the complete heroic contrast to
the false Mrs. Donnelly in the medicine show who bawls at her son John:

> Then you're no son of mine. Until you've killed your man the way your
> darling father did, you're no son of mine.
>
> [p. 24]

The true Mrs. Donnelly hides her husband for almost two years from the constables. She petitions for the commutation of his sentence, teaches Will his catechism and initiates him into the Donnelly's sense of self-worth. She gives Will a fiddle for his birthday, an instrument he plays so jubilantly that he is able to face down a mob simply by playing ''Boney over the Alps,'' in ''The St. Nicholas Hotel.'' As a mother, Mrs. Donnelly is loving and fair. Still, there is one characteristic before all others: her ability to stand alone, and turn the tide of events, with only the force of her will. Time and again, friends and enemies of the Donnellys exclaim:

> Judith Donnelly who were once Judith Magee. You alone of anyone here can save my brother. Tell them to stop.
>
> [p. 41]

> Faced with Donnelly's wife, however, they signed their names or made their marks to the truth at last. I shall bring the truth out of Biddulph yet and my husband alive back some day to his seven children and his farm.
>
> [p. 36]

> My wife, Tom, is the only person in the settlement who ever stood up to you. She stopped you from cutting up Donegan and until she's afraid and wants to leave I'm not either. . . .
>
> [p. 50]

The tragic undercurrent of these remarks is such precisely because the Donnellys, led by Mrs. Donnelly, have this formidable will; the family alone is strong enough to bring the truth out of Biddulph. A weaker family might have fled, or made peace with the Whitefeet, but the indomitable Donnellys stay on in the township, preparing to meet their inevitable destiny. The truth in Biddulph is that the Whitefeet are not left behind in the old country and that the Donnellys are marked as Blackfoot traitors to the society even in the New World. As Blackfeet, the family is trapped in the mire of the Irish feud, and as Donnellys the family is strong enough to discover the true extent of hatred and violence in Biddulph.

When identifying the Donnellys with the process of the seasons, I was trying to name the quality that allows them to be passionately violent at one moment and tranquil and reflective the next. They are not a natural force in the way a storm rages and subsides. But the idea of the calm acceptance of a seasonal pattern, which Mr. Donnelly sees in the fortunes of his family comes close to the steady process of growth in their new farm, interrupted briefly by death, imprisonment, violence and then continuing with more growth, more sons, more wheat. In this world the natural of the Donnellys is not George Stub, who, as a storekeeper in the village of Lucan, is too different to be a true opposite, but Tom Cassleigh, the leader of the Whitefoot faction among the Biddulph

Catholics. Cassleigh is as powerful among these people as George Stub is in the village. As the keeper of the secret flame of vengeance fired in Ireland after Mr. Donnelly refused to join the Whitefeet, Cassleigh is their worst enemy. George Stub can use his legal position to taunt them with arrests and mock trials. Cassleigh, through his authority as the new Matthew Midnight, is able to turn the other Irish Catholics — their own people — against the Donnellys.

Both Mr. and Mrs. Donnelly have face to face confrontations with Cassleigh, and both defeat him for the moment. Mrs. Donnelly saves the life of a man Cassleigh is torturing at a logging bee. In a suggestion of the symmetry possible in the regions of Biddulph, the man she saves is the brother of Sarah Farl, the wife of the man Mr. Donnelly killed at a logging bee in 1857. Mrs. Donnelly, in an effort to receive the forgiveness of Sarah Farl, goes out to stop Cassleigh and his gang:

> Have you, Mr. Cassleigh, tortured him enough? Put that knife back where it belongs, Mr. Cassleigh, if you still know what pockets are for, or do you carry the knife permanently stuck in your hand like a thorn? *Cassleigh comes towards her with his knife, but her glance forces him to weave out from the wheel, through it, and around the barnyard.* Get back you, savage . . .
>
> [p. 42]

The monstrosity and unnaturalness of Cassleigh is emphasized again and again in his confrontation with Mr. Donnelly. In this case, it is the day following the burning of the Donnelly's barn and Cassleigh, smug and secure in his new post as the first Catholic Justice of the Peace in Biddulph, threatens Donnelly with further violence if he does not accept this last offer to enlist with his seven sons in the Whitefeet. Donnelly refuses to kneel or swear again, and whips the new wagon and Cassleigh down the Roman Line to show who is still master of the road that Donnelly built. The strange intensity of this scene is reinforced by the absolute stillness of the stage as the two men scowl back and forth. *Sticks and Stones* is usually a full canvas of the pioneer life, but in this case it is quiet and empty as the mortal enemies meet at the crossroads, no one in sight for miles around. A mental theatre, or a battle of wills is present in the Cassleigh/Donnelly dialogue, which reaches its height not when Donnelly whips off the wagon or when Cassleigh threatens Donnelly with the return of the Whitefeet to his door. Rather, the centre of the match, and the centre of the play, is reached when Mr. Donnelly compares himself with Cassleigh:

> Aye, I killed, shure I killed—fighting for my name and my family and my land in hot blood. On this very road down at the tracks you killed—by cold proxy. Having myself seven sons and a girl I ask what children have you? What have you got between your legs, Cassleigh — a knife? . . .
>
> [p. 50]

Here is the seasonal opposition at the heart of the play. Donnelly is the hot blooded vital summer, and Cassleigh, the cold frost of sterility (what children?), winter, monstrosity (first the thorn in hand, now the knife between the legs). In politics they are Blackfoot and Whitefoot, but before and beyond this, Donnelly and Cassleigh are two archetypal forces battling over the new land; the one for growth and plenty, the other for destruction and waste. Thus, if one steps back from the debate about the goodness/badness of the Donnellys, another play emerges. This hidden work, a documentary and epic about pioneer life in Upper Canada, the Canadian equivalent of the western, showing the transformation of the wilderness into a garden, is the universal story of the Donnellys. The problems faced by the Donnellys, (bad-hearted neighbors, difficulties in establishing the validity of their title to the farm, inability to escape the old world) are all frontier commonplaces. For the Donnellys, however, these problems are not simply related to the usual jostling in a new community: the struggles of the Donnellys are a concerted effort by their enemies to keep the sticks and stones of the title from building up a secure farmhouse. In the theatre of James Reaney, where words are so frequently more damaging than deeds, a man called a Blackfoot *is* a blackfoot, an alien, to be treated as cruelly as any monster.

Mrs Donnelly	Mr. Donnelly, there's a proverb that sticks and stones may hurt my bones, but words will never harm them.
Mr Donnelly	Not true, Mrs. Donnelly. Not true at all. If only he'd hit us with a stone or a stick, but ever since that day you told me they'd been calling our son that in the churchyard it's as if a thousand little tinkly pebbles keep batting up against the windows in my mind just when it's a house that's about to sleep . . .

[p. 22]

Two of the children, Jennie and Will, try to lead their parents away from the grinding of the sticks and the stones, the echoes of the nights of fire and blood in Ireland. Will, the heir to the spirit of his parents nearly fiddles his enemies into submission, even as a child. Jennie, who leaves Biddulph for the town of St. Thomas upon her marriage, resembles Owen in that she too is trying to dream it out, to seek the happy ending in dreams that she fears will be denied her in Biddulph. So, the play ends with Jennie recounting a dream, in which her parents almost leave the township. But the Donnellys delay over the wash, the dog . . . and finally even the dream ends, as the play does with Mrs. Donnelly saying, prophetic and matter-of-fact: "Jennie, your father and I will never leave Biddulph." [p. 51] Jennie sums up the verbal imagery of the play in a major speech shortly before this:

Two of us were old enough to see what had happened. Patrick left when he married, so did I. Old enough, coward enough, I mean. We could see that we could never join that Church that the bishop had finally come to with fire for a mitre and a torch for a crook and had not just slapped us all lightly on either cheek as token for sufferings we must endure as followers of Jesus, no — the old ruffian had knocked us on the floor, to the floor, and kicked us with his hooved boot and punched us with thistle mitts and said: get the hell out, you bugger Donnellys. No water for you, but we've fire.

[p. 50]

So the Donnellys are not confirmed as anything other than Donnellys. The children, whose ages have formed one of the narrative components of the story, are now old enough to die with their parents or coward enough to leave the township and tell the tale from a safer distance. The spiritual life of the Irish has invaded the natural and seasonal existence of the Donnellys. The bishop, the thresher, the unnatural Cassleigh (surely the thistle mitts are his) have joined into one mob because the Donnellys, John Barleycorn, the summer, must die. The Donnelly's barn is burned in the fall of 1867, the year of Confederation. In Biddulph, there is a secret conspiracy formed for the purpose of driving out the Donnellys, a confederation of blood and midnight allegiance. As the Donnelly's barn blazes in the autumn night, the sense of winter is in the air, of an end to the harvest, and an imprisonment of the land.

The mime and action throughout the play magnifies this aura of advancing despair: the dominant motif of the Tarragon production was the intersection of huge diagonals across the stage from the corner, back through the middle, and down to the opposite corner. This symbolic movement recurs in the form of Mr. Donnelly's mark, his signature and claim to his land; as the hint of the unexpected confines of Biddulph, not a freely formed paradise at all but sometimes simply one dark room; and ultimately, as the St. Patrick's cross, the sign of Ireland, which the characters, in their efforts to escape or reform, only find themselves retracing and repeating. This combination of imagery (verbal and visual) provides the core of Reaney's explanation. The night in Ireland when Mr. Donnelly stepped outside to refuse the Whitefeet, lead, inevitably, to the murder of his family forty years later in Canada. The strength of character that made it possible for Mr. Donnelly to assert his independence in the suspicious world of Ireland so inflamed those suspicions that his death became a necessity.

The Donnelly family are thrust into the Run of the Arrow during their thirty-six years in Biddulph. The more they assert their right to a civilized life free from the turbulence and savagery of the world around them, the more the Donnellys find themselves forced to fight back. The range of activity that Reaney uses to depict the Donnelly fight for independence is necessarily large. The story could not be told otherwise. Like the wild Irishmen in Kelley's book, actors must sing, dance, fight, or chant, mime, hum. The language of the play, with its numerous quotations and vigorous replies reflects a society which has turned everyone into witnesses. All the characters must clear their names somehow, and repeat the truth as they know it. There is even a hint of pessimism as to the ability of the writing to tell the whole story: Mr. Donnelly alludes to the difficulty in telling his story, even as he is asserting his legal right to his land:

> *but kneeling on only one knee*
> Now my body belongs to its dust
> Which dust once belonged to me.
> As it is blown away, I forget
> Concession Six Lot Eighteen
> South Half or North Half which was mine?
> We are blown away and both lost *prayer stops*
> > Like actor's words.

[p. 19]

To someone following the entire development of James Reaney's career as a dramatist, this is a moving moment. Beyond the image of the dispersal of the Donnelly's consciousness with their murder, there is a brief glimpse of Reaney's own feelings about his life as a playwright. The plays that started out as almost all words, all poetry, have been replaced by a different sort of drama, and suddenly there is a sense of loss; even the major speeches may no longer succeed in threading out the whole of the tapestry. Mr. Donnelly immediately melts into the chorus and the medicine show with the Black Donnellys arrives noisily off stage, and the story is resumed: but the moment lingers. For an instant we have seen the tale broken up by second thoughts from the teller.

Notes to Chapter Nine

1. Kelley, Thomas, *The Black Donnellys*, (Don Mills: Greywood, 1954).

2. Reaney, James. *Sticks and Stones The Donnellys, Part One*, (Erin: Press Porcépic, 1975). Unless noted otherwise, all references are drawn from this edition.

3. Miller, Orlo. *The Donnellys Must Die*, (Toronto: Macmillan of Canada, 1972).

4. " . . . Then you meet a local minister who writes a book counter to the grisly version which has by now become enshrined in a penny dreadful called *The Black Donnellys*. According to the local minister the family were not quite so black; in fact, according to him they're almost innocent; not quite, but they had a door anyhow; were the subjects of a great deal of slander and lies and we tend to see them through their enemies' eyes. Aha, a double point of view! A mystery! One starts doing one's own research . . . " Reaney, James. "Some Questions and Some Answers."

5. *Saga of Njal*, translated by Magnusson and Pálssen, (London: Penguin, 1960).

---

6. Miller, Orlo. *The Donnellys Must Die*, (Toronto: Macmillan of Canada, 1972), p. 102.

7. Frye, Northrop. "Quest and Cycle in *Finnegans Wake*" from *Fables of Identity; Studies in Poetic Mythology*, (New York: Harcourt, Brace and World, 1963), p. 257.

8. Orlo Miller records that by 1878 the signatures on a petition for the release of Bob Donnelly were, with a few exceptions, those of Prostestants.

Miller, Orlo. *The Donnellys Must Die*, (Toronto: Macmillan of Canada, 1972), p. 138.

10

Listen to the Wind

> What is theatre? A kind of cybernetic machine. When it is not working,
> this machine is hidden behind a curtain. But as soon as it is revealed, it
> begins emitting a certain number of messages. These messages have this
> peculiarity, that they are simultaneous and yet of a different rhythm; at a
> certain point in the performance, you receive at the same time six or seven
> items of information . . . What we have, then, is a real informational
> polyphony, which is what theatricality is: *a density of signs* (in relation to
> literary monody and leaving aside the question of cinema). . . . [1]

Whether or not James Reaney would concur with this definition of the theatre, it
is certain that the extensive changes in the character of his work following
Listen to the Wind[2] may partly be understood on the basis of semiology.
Previous to its debut in 1966, Reaney's work in the theatre could be read as long
poems, with the thrust of character and setting carried almost exclusively by the
dialogue. Occasional bursts of another type of dramatic activity—the escape of
Madam Fay, weasel-like from the courtroom, for example—were sufficiently
isolated to qualify as exceptional rather than routine. In *Listen to the Wind*,
however, a whole range of sign-systems are used freely and co-operatively to
create the worlds of 1936, Perth County and 1870, Caresfoot Court. The usual
density of language is replaced by a reduced naturalism in the Perth County
sequences and a deliberate use of "melodramatic" material in "The Saga of
Caresfoot Court." Also mixed in with the kinds of verbal language are songs
(Green Gravel); poetry of the Brontë children chanted by the chorus; a spontaneous Carl Orff-derived system of musical accompaniment and ono-
matopoeic sound effects. A certain system of signification allows the pair of
antlers carried across the stage by a leaping child to signify the forest, or the
pale blue sheet shaking gently between two chairs signifies the stream in the
forest; a self-conscious theatricality which allows Owen to instruct the chorus

> No—that's the Mediterranean. Madeira is in the Atlantic.
> *Chorus*:
> *setting up potted palm and making louder sea sounds*

Owen:
No, no, this is the Atlantic near the Equator.
Chorus:
They adjust their sea sounds and also mime gramophone.

[Act II, Sc. xxxvii]

It is a system of direct discourse with the audience so that we are kept informed of set changes and even observe some of the changes that the children decide to make in the course of the performance. Finally, there are several different types of acting: one for the farmhouse in 1936 which is muted and played down so that strong gestures (such as Mrs. Taylor drinking tea straight from the tea-pot spout) are the moments of outstanding intensity; another, more violent and forceful action and language and death. Beyond this, the acting necessary in the choral scenes in which the actors must in a sense step back from the action, as Angela and Arthur do in their poetic love scenes which are controlled by the pattern of the sign-systems. My choice of *Listen to the Wind* as James Reaney's major work in the theatre is a confirmation of my feeling that the catalogue of devices listed here is fully controlled by his imaginative powers, and by the fact that his control over the material in no way prevents the play from being one of his most idiosyncratic. *Listen to the Wind* combines personal control with experimental daring in a new way for Reaney, and the play is delightful to read, think about, or watch any time at all.

The idiosyncracy of the work is confirmed in the choice of H. Rider Haggard's *Dawn* as the source, the play-within-a-play. Many of the best lines in *Listen to the Wind* are drawn directly from the novel, and while it does not have the same strength of meaning for me that it holds for my father, it is quite possible to see something of the power inside it that he sees.[3] Furthermore, it is possible to guess at the reasons why setting large chunks of *Dawn* on the stage would appeal to Reaney. A never-to-be-underestimated motive is the element of self-conscious defiance involved in adapting so adamantly a "melodramatic" work. *Dawn* is a novel in which the good are exalted or rewarded faithfully, and the bad killed or told off in several delightful ways, and the basic excitement of the original plot is reproduced with some adjustments in *Listen to the Wind*. Reaney's second and deeper intention to demonstrate the power that the strong situation of the novel holds for him is borne out in the closeness of the plot in "The Saga of Caresfoot Court" to *Dawn*: Phillip (Piers in the play to connect him with Canada's own 'Jalna') really does kill his father by refusing to give his father, Devil Caresfoot, the medicine the old man needs. Angela really does marry Arthur despite marrying George (Douglas in the play) first. Geraldine, Lady Bellamy in the novel, and George do conspire to convince Angela that Arthur has died. Piers agrees to separate the young lovers so that this conspiracy may proceed, hoping to win back the lands Douglas gained from him by the terms of his father's will. The adjustments that are made are most significant, as they turn the Rider Haggard material into something else. The Douglas/Geraldine subplot (if this phrase is ever applicable to Reaney's work) is developed into the love/hate relationship of the play, and the detail of the murdered child added. Haggard uses a great deal of the second half of the novel to discuss Arthur in Madeira, and the woman he meets there, while in the play this is reduced to one small fragment. Phillip Caresfoot is an unattractive figure throughout *Dawn*; murdering his father, cursing his dying wife, betraying his only child to his cousin, and Haggard attributes these crimes to his boundless avarice. In "The Saga of Caresfoot Court," the starving dogs he rounds up for the medical school compounded his avarice. Another smaller change illustrates the loving/amused care with which Reaney has rebuilt the structure of *Dawn* into his play. In the original, the name of Phillip's German wife is Hilda von Holtzhausen, and the part she plays in *Listen to the Wind* contains many of the identical lines. Her name in the play, however, is Claudia von Yorick, and given her new Danish ancestry, this is evidently a *Hamlet* joke, whatever Rider Haggard might have thought. The most important change of all is introduced most casually. Phillip and George are bitter enemies, but they are cousins, and George is the son of a weak-willed brother of Devil Caresfoot. Piers is the legal heir in "The Saga of Caresfoot Court," it is said just as the children start to produce the play.

"Douglas is—no one knows who his father is . . . " [Act I, Sc. iii] With this apparently inconsequential change in ancestry we enter the world of what is avowedly Reaney's favorite novel, *Wuthering Heights*,[4] and we begin to see the outlines of the young Heathcliff and Hindley Earnshaw fighting over the future of the Heights. Once this adjustment in focus is made, we start to perceive a whole play about the Brontës taking shape out of the seemingly disassociated Perth County and Caresfoot Court material. Jay Macpherson (in her preface to the *Talonbooks* edition) and Alvin Lee fill in the areas of Brontë reference in the two worlds. This turns up in small details such as the changing of names as Arthur's dog, Aleck, becomes the Brontë's dog, Keeper or the nurse, Piggott, becomes Tabby or Martha. Similarly the fight with the pillows between Angela and Arthur recalls the rather vigorous game of ball played by Catherine Linton and Linton Heathcliff in *Wuthering Heights*:

> . . . he consented to play at ball with me. We found two in a cupboard, among a heap of old toys: tops, and hoops, and battledores, and shuttlecocks. One was marked C., and the other H.; I wished to have the C., because that stood for Catherine, and the H. might be for Heathcliff, his name; but the bran came out of H., and Linton didn't like that.
>
> I beat him constantly; and he got cross again, and coughed, and returned to his chair. . . . [5]

The contact and infrequent visits made between the Heights and the Grange are parallelled by the wanderings back and forth in ''The Saga of Caresfoot Court.'' Arthur is a ward of Douglas in *Dawn*, while in the play he is the son of Maria Lawry, the fiancée of Piers, until his impulsive decision to marry Claudia. In another motif analagous to the northland heights, the marriage of Angela and Arthur resolves the quarrel between their estates as the marriage of Cathy Linton and Hareton Earnshaw resolves the tempestuous pattern of *Wuthering Heights*. The character of Rogue does not appear in *Dawn*, and his treatment by Douglas suggests Heathcliff's treatment of the young Hareton in his work as Heathcliff's assistant. At one point, the material qualifies as an homage to the Brontë novel. Angela asks Mr. Gleneden, '' . . . what lies over there behind those hills? Beyond the forest. Is it the sea?'' [Act I, Sc. xxiv] She directly echoes Cathy Linton asking Ellen the same question. Another use of Brontë material to transform the structure of *Dawn* is the adaptation of Emily Brontë's poetic cycle *Gondal's Queen*[6] (''a novel in verse'') into the Geraldine/Douglas subplot. Rider Haggard kept this relationship quite shadowy and subservient to the romance of Arthur and Angela. Throughout ''The Saga of Caresfoot Court,'' there is a full range of scenes involving the Douglas/Geraldine affair which operate in counterpoint to the romance. In the novel, Haggard hints that Geraldine abandoned her husband and child and has remained infatuated with Douglas ever since. A darker version is told in the play: Geraldine murders the child she had by Douglas, and the letters Douglas holds over as revenge for murdering a part of him concern her efforts to choke the infant. These changes are derived from the world of *Gondal's Queen* which narrates the rise to eminence of Geraldine Almeda in the imaginary South Sea kingdom of Gondal. Ruthless and selfish with her lovers as éhe changes of fortune dictate, Geraldine abandons an infant child with the defeat in battle of one of her champions. There is, however, one overriding lover in her life, Julius Brenzaida. With the encouragement of Geraldine, Julius unsurps the throne of Gondal and rules for a time as Emperor. A conspiracy brings about the assassination of Julius, leaving Geraldine to rule alone. Able to continue as Empress for a dozen years, Geraldine is herself assassinated by a band of outlaws led by the daughter of Lord Elbe, a husband she had thrown over for Julius. Many of the names in ''The Saga of Caresfoot Court'' are drawn from this work, as the names Fraser, Carr, Bellamy change to Gleneden, Elbe, Eldred and so on. Implicit in the *Gondal* material is the establishment of Geraldine as a Queen of power, as she avenges the death of her father, the Charlatan. In the original, Geraldine used her dark magic to advance the cause of Douglas because of her love/hate for Douglas. The compulsion for her intervention in the lives of the Caresfoots is more complex in the play. There is the new element of revenge and also the additional curse of her dead child which compels her to be ''seven long years a wolf in the woods.'' [Act I, Sc. vii] A further refinement of the Geraldine strands of plot in *Dawn* allows

Reaney to present a more complex relationship with Angela. The novel turns on the basic irony of her infatuation with Douglas. At the height of her powers, Geraldine is forced to scheme so that the man she loves may marry a young rival of hers. Haggard implies a tentative resolution in the Geraldine/Angela conflict, as Angela with the assistance of Lady Bellamy, finds Arthur in Madeira. *Dawn* ends happily with Arthur and Angela united through this beneficial intervention of Geraldine. "The Saga of Caresfoot Court" also concludes with the young lovers united again, but the resolution is achieved in a more profound fashion, as will be seen later on.

The Brontë material extends from the world below, back into the Perth County scenes, and this region of the play has been admirably illuminated by Jay Macpherson and Alvin Lee. A person only a little familiar with the lives of the Brontës would sense the connection between Owen, Harriet, Jenny, and Ann dreaming it out through their play; and Branwell, Emily, Charlotte and Anne putting on their Young Men's Plays and working on their poetry. As Alvin Lee reveals, the connections extend further:

> The influence of the Brontës on Reaney's play is pronounced. Like the four Brontë children who survived childhood — Branwell, Charlotte, Emily, and Anne—Reaney's boy and three girls are isolated; deprived of adequate parental love, and gifted with extraordinary powers of fancy. Like the Brontës, Owen and the girls get help in "listening to the wind" from four adults: a doctor, a housekeeper, a father, and a sexton. The last three are readily identifiable from the Brontë story. Tabby — she has the same name in Reaney's play — as in Haworth parsonage — is the old Brontë servant and nurse. There is the father, always in the background helping to feed the imaginations of the children but, in his massive self-sufficiency, not really taking care of their emotional needs. And Mitch, Owen's crony, who takes care of the church, is based on John Brown, the Haworth sexton, stonemason, gravedigger and highly intelligent friend of Branwell Brontë. Owen, at one point bellowing out Tarzan lines and at another crying for his mother's arms, is Branwell Brontë in his dual role as a Gondal character who lives hard, loves desperately, and dies cursing, but who cannot make real life measure up to his fantasies. . . . [7]

Once the nature of this tribute to the Brontës is established, the correspondence between the worlds of Perth County and Caresfoot Court emerge from the apparent separation of the two states. In the real time and space of Perth County in 1936 are the Brontë figures of the children and their friends, creating and imagining in isolation from the fashionable cultural and literary salons of the day. The world below is the land that the Brontës created in their childhood, stretching from the bleak northland heights to the south Pacific and vibrant with love, hate, confusion, death, new life emotion. Beyond this extensive *homage* to the Brontës is another story which uses this biography and creativity to narrate the sickness and despair of Owen's existence and his efforts to create a world and art appropriate to the life he feels ebbing away from him. In this regard the quick discussion of Tarzan (a figure far more heroic and mysterious to Reaney than anyone familiar only with the Johnny Weissmuller travesties might imagine) signals a suddenness and vitality that subsides just as quickly. Owen doesn't want a " . . . special language . . . a glossary in the back." [Act I, Sc. i] What he wants is a metaphor for the languid and powerless life that he is leading as his parents separate and his illness approaches crisis. Owen's choice of "The Saga of Caresfoot Court" as a suitable subject for the summer play is made in the knowledge that aside from expressing his own sense of despair, it is also the novel his father gave his mother shortly before they were married, and he has already cast his mother as Geraldine. Owen only conceals for a short time his hope that this renewed involvement of his mother in the life of the Taylor home in a work for which she has a sentimental attachment will somehow affect a reconciliation in his parents' marriage. As touching as this idea might appear, it is foredoomed, considering the roles taken by his parents in the play. These roles represent bitter distortions of their actual lives as Mr. Taylor plays Edward Eldred, the country attorney thrust into prominence by Geraldine (Mrs. Taylor) in her efforts to make Douglas the master of Caresfoot Court. Eldred is by no means a forceful character in "The Saga of Caresfoot Court" and joins the conspiracy against Angela and Arthur so that he may read the dark letters Geraldine wrote to Douglas about their child. Eldred's big speech of revenge as he reveals that he has already studied the letters, and so may destroy Geraldine:

From this moment on you are a ruined woman. A penniless outcast. For years I've longed to have revenge on you for the humilities you've made me suffer. And now —

is cut short of satisfaction by Geraldine's scornful reply:

Edward, get back in the mud where you belong. The mud where I found you — a bumbling pitiful little country attorney — whom I made Sir Eldred. . . .

[Act II, Sc. xliii]

Toward the end of the play this exchange is reflected in the dimension of the lives of the Taylors as it is made apparent where the psychic power in their marriage is located:

Father:
Are you going to stay?

Mother:
Don't be silly. Of course not. Surely you don't want me to stay.
Father:
You're going to ride off now on my best horse.
Mother:
Of course. Try and stop me. That horse obeys my whistle and not yours.
By the way — could you tell Owen to keep cutting off those thorns on the
locust trees in the orchard. The little colts can kill themselves if they get
pressed against them.

[Act III, Sc. xlv, xlvi, and xlvii]

As usual in the works of Reaney, the greatest evil is committed in the most
childish and casual manner. Thus, the Taylors are able to squabble over their
horses, instead of putting their differences to one side for the night and trying to
save Owen. At this desperate moment in the life of their son, they choose to part
with assertions of suspicion and ego ("that horse obeys my whistle"). The
alienation in their marriage has so progressed that the last words about the horse
and the colts and the thorns assume a bitterly ironic quality. Owen's parents still
have reservoirs of love and affection, but these are misplaced and thoughtless.
For Reaney, the competition over the horses symbolizes the dead end of
realism. In this case reality is not pushed to the absurd but to the mundane. So,
the dramatic reconciliation that Owen dreams of is not possible in the "real"
world of Perth County, given the restricted unemotional life together his
parents are ending.
    That the reconciliation does happen in the world below with the engagement
ball rejoining Arthur and Angela, contrasts the power of play and imagination
with the very unmelodramatic reality. Toward the end of *Listen to the Wind*
there is considerable emphasis placed on the intimations of invincibility and
immortality of this imaginative world. In one sense this is happening because
Owen is becoming progressively more ill, less able to cope with the real world,
which seems to be dissolving into the petty bickering of his parents' marriage or
the wider more fearful despair of his sickness. At one point, he retreats into his
childhood:

Mother and father. It is time that you are together again. I felt you both
touching me — like rain. I'm not very old yet, you know. I still want to be
held. If you keep letting go of me — I'll slip away.

[Act II, Sc. xli]

Owen does slip away into the delirium of the world below as the barren
surface reality becomes less and less a handhold into eternity. This delirium is a
triumph of the imagination as Owen's metaphor replaces the dreary reality, and

it is victoriously possible to dream out the "happy ending" that Owen so longs for.

There is a pessimistic corollary to this triumph, however. Rather than the triumph of the theatre over the difficulties of production, the reconciliation of Arthur and Angela is attached to a deep fatalism that hints such victories cost the winner all there is to give. Owen, the deepest dreamer, who sails to the eternity of his creation also dies a tragic, needless death because of his increasing (and necessary) preoccupation with his dream. Sometimes the dreamer cannot wake up, and if the "world below" leaves Ann with memories years later of a past she will not lose, it demands the final charge of passage for others.

The "world below" the four children create and enter during their summer together is at once the subconscious, vivid universe which is the locale of so many of Reaney's plays and the four royal houses around Caresfoot Court. As a voyage through the subconscious fears and desires of the four children, the play functions as a "sophisticated form of psychodrama."[8] The play opens with the three girls advancing through the audience tossing a ball back and forth, but once they arrive at the Taylors', they leave the ball-tossing behind and immediately begin to discuss the collapse of their families.[9] Only Jenny can reply to Owen's question about the parents, "together as can be." [Act I, Sc. i] Harriet and Ann are both in the same position as Owen, with their parents separated for the summer at least. Owen has the most intense feelings about the separation of his parents, and the other children follow his lead into Caresfoot Court: as their fathers and mothers come to resemble witches and devils, they need the spiritual unity of the resilient form of the play-within-a-play. The fragmentation of their families is set in opposition to the relations of the four families, "The Saga of Caresfoot Court" presents the opportunity to rebuild the fragmentary disorder of their actual lives into the imaginative circles/mandalas that are the dominant feature of the Caresfoot stage.

Once the families in the play-within-a-play are arranged in a system moving from the darkest (physically and morally) to the fairest, a chain like this develops:

ALMEDA::CARESFOOT::LAWRY::von YORICK

An examination of the relations among the houses reveals a world in which there are zones of love and war, healing the wounds or tearing the families apart. The Almedas wage a war of revenge upon the Caresfoots as Geraldine punishes the heirs of Devil Caresfoot for the death of her father. Yet there is also a tortuous love affair, complete with the murdered child as Geraldine and George act out the dark, obsessed bottom of the play. The power of the Almedas is irrational and mystic, while the property and title of Caresfoot Court allow Devil Caresfoot to exercise his authority as local gentry and drive out the Charlatan. Ironically, the legal force of the Caresfoot's destroys the family as Piers attempts to reclaim his title by circumventing the terms of his father's will. Little is revealed of the Lawry family, although the marriage of Piers to Maria (and her meadows) that Devil longs for would represent the self-interested combination of title and property that the Caresfoot family continually seeks to acquire. Thus, the impetuous decision by Piers to marry Claudia von Yorick causes an ironic separation of property and title. In marrying Claudia instead of Maria, Piers chooses love over self-interest: Claudia is the final scion of her Danish noble house but has none of the property that Maria is to be willed. The ironic reversal arises as Devil, in his will, strips Piers of everything but the title of Squire Caresfoot; in other words, the secret marriage to Claudia leaves Piers as Squire Caresfoot in name only, and it is the cuckoo bird, Douglas, who inherits the family lands. Douglas, however, is not satisfied to be a landed country notable, and his desire to become the next Squire Caresfoot represents a parallel to the ambition of Geraldine to enter into the society of the Caresfoots and the Lawrys. This driving ambition is a measure of the horrors of the world below. Geraldine murders her child; Piers sacrifices his daughter; Devil disinherits his son; actions that are all taken in an effort to affect material fortunes. As balance to this bitter materialism there is the spiritual good fortune flowing outward from the von Yorick house. If Piers destroys his financial future by marrying Claudia, their daughter Angela provides the wholesome power capable of transforming a world disfigured by the sorcery of the Almedas and the brutish greed of the Caresfoots. Angela is initially cursed by Piers since her sex delivered him into the grip of his father's will. Had Claudia's child been a boy, Piers would have remained the guardian of the family estates. Although he betrays her to Douglas and Geraldine so that he may regain the lost lands, Angela survives his cruelty. She is as far above him as her mother, Claudia, was, yet it is somehow dramatically ennobling that, at least once, a Caresfoot placed love before money. The impetuous and secret marriage which broke up the self-interested engagement of Piers and Maria is demonically parodied by the rape of Maria's daughter by Douglas:

> Brenzeida had a younger sister—I came across her in the forest one day and got that (Rogue) for my pains. Nine months later.
>
> [Act II, Sc. xxxix]

Douglas and Piers form a completed image of the Caresfoot family. One is choked with avarice and collects stray dogs for a living, while the other is a wild huntsman, savage and brutal. Piers is destroyed by Angela because he joins as tacit conspirator in the plotting of Geraldine and Douglas and invites the wrath of God called down by Claudia in her dying prayer:

> . . . My motherless babe. May the power of God protect you. Angels guard you. And may the curse of God fall upon those who would bring evil

upon you. Piers, you have heard my words. In your charge I leave the child. See that you never betray the trust.

[Act I, Sc. xxi]

Divine retribution does fall upon the conspirators. Piers is devoured by his dogs; Douglas is killed by Geraldine, and Geraldine herself is thwarted in her suicide attempt. This considerable string of ill fortune may be taken as proof that within the confines of the world below, the greatest power is that of the von Yoricks. Geraldine engages in a staring match with Claudia when they first meet, and this strong attraction/repulsion hints at the underlying relation between Geraldine and Angela. Geraldine is the wolf in the woods and suc-ceeds in destroying all that she wishes; Angela, conversely, is a victim of Geraldine's machinations from her birth and yet survives to exhibit a force to which even Geraldine is beholden. Claudia shields Angela with comb and ring, heirlooms of some ancient white magic. The comb with the star radiant upon it is especially a force of protective good, found by Arthur in the forest and then taken away from Angela again by Douglas on their wedding night. Angela is also protected by the lunar dominion of her mother. As Arthur and Angela sail their small boats of candle and bark down the forest stream, Angela's boat disappears into the water:

Oh, Arthur—my candle's drowned. But the moon shall be my candle and she is brighter now than the day.

[Act II, Sc. xxxii]

Claudia is set against Geraldine, whose power is drawn from the deepest regions of the space. Her astronomical candle is the evil winking star of Algor, and her power dark and cold, like those far reaches of the galaxy. Although Angela and Geraldine are even more in opposition than Claudia and Geraldine, as they are the motherless babe and the child murderer, there is, nevertheless, a powerful connection between their two lives:

I might have given this talisman of my power to Angela if she could have sworn never to continue her love for that wretched weakling, Arthur Brenzaida. But I know how loving and weak her heart is. . . .

[Act III, Sc. xlv, xlvi, and xlvii]

Despite her scorn for this weak and loving nature, which means that her secret knowledge of the universe (''mesmerism'') will die with her, Geraldine is ultimately dependent on the forgiveness of Angela. In an effort to rid herself of the ghost-child who haunts her, Geraldine has given Angela a doll with the child's wishbone sewn into its body. Angela refuses to love the doll, and for many years Geraldine is tormented by guilt. Only after Geraldine has destroyed her life, as she once destroyed her mother, is Angela finally capable of loving the doll, and thus releasing Geraldine. In a last ironic reversal, Geraldine, who has controlled so many lives, attempts suicide, and for once her magic fails her. She lives on, paralyzed and full of hatred for the life she longs to leave until, as the ghost-child relates:

> Your wish is granted. You've been a wolf in the forest twice times seven years and now you will be freed. *Angela kisses the doll.* For at last some one good enough has been found to kiss the rag doll you made of my bones —loving enough to lick the sores of Lazarus and gentle enough to weep for the scorpion. Farewell, I have found at last my true mother. The West Wind blows and lights the Evening Star.
>
> [Act III, Sc. xlviii]

Previous to this act of liberation is another image connecting Geraldine with Angela. When Geraldine informed Douglas of her reasons for murdering their child, she referred to the child as an obstacle in the path of her ambitions for herself and Douglas:

> . . . Douglas, there is within me a Spirit of Power that I've always known was mine ever since I helped my father with his mesmerism. That Spirit, Douglas, is a river in jail as things now stand. You'll be a game keeper the rest of your life.

Moments before she finally does kiss the doll, Angela cries out:

> Which of the twelve winds of Heaven shall blow it (the evil star of Algor) out? The West Wind! The West Wind! Oh come and help me free the prisoner, the river frozen in the jail of winter.
>
> [Act III, Sc. xlviii]

Earlier in this invocation/plea by Angela, Algor has been placed in its astronomical position: it is the tooth in the head of Medusa held by Perseus. The suggestion here is that Geraldine is monstrous (the epithet of so many of the early plays) and unnatural. She is the killing spirit, the poisonous winter of the play who is paradoxically the victim of her own evil. Geraldine can only find peace through the intervention of the fairytale princess she has hounded so cruelly.

Geraldine justifies her cruelty in these words to Piers Caresfoot shortly before he is devoured by the starving dogs. Piers is so paralyzed with haunting guilt that he is unable to rise from his chair as Geraldine binds him:

> Well, Squire Caresfoot. Long ago your father told the village constable to whip my father out of the village. He died in a ditch that night, I his poor

daughter by. Now it's time the Caresfoots paid all of their debt to the Almedas. Oh you are worse than I am—I bit and scratched to save my life, but you sold a beautiful young girl to get back your clay. I knew you'd do it. And now that you've done it I know I must kill you for it. Like the Christians' God I tempt and if you fall — I destroy. . . .

[Act III, sc. xlv, xlvi and xlvii]

As is usual with the villains in Reaney's plays, they are motivated by two drives: the first to enter into society as equals, and the second to resolve an inner tension caused by an intensive metaphysic which compels them to follow a pattern of destruction in their lives. (One thinks, for example, of Bethel Henry working out her feelings about the nature of good and evil.) Geraldine is similar to the other powers of evil in that she desires to break into the homes of the wealthy and acts her role of Destruction in her role as God. These twin compulsions result in paradox: to marry Attorney Eldred, she must murder her child, and, because of this murder, she is at the mercy of the daughter of her rival, Angela. In trapping Piers in his chair, Geraldine is ironically fulfilling the terms of Claudia's dying prayer for the protection of Angela, another case in which the mutual connection is brought to the fore, undercutting the surface opposition of Geraldine and Angela.

The nature of this connection may be established in reference to the proof of the existence of God shared with Owen by Mitch. Owen is filled with despair and says of God that sometimes (in the case of his own life, for example) he seems the evilest person around. Mitch replies conventionally at first:

Mitch:
You musn't say that Owen. He died for you on the cross.
Owen:
He — the older one didn't Mitch. He made the tree that the cross was cut out of, don't forget.

[Act III, Sc. xliv]

Faced with the suspicions of Owen, Mitch replies to his doubts a second time, this time by parable. Mitch tells Owen that one weekend when feeling rather low, he attempted suicide by drinking all that remained in each and every bottle of his grandmother's medicine cabinet. Despite consuming everything from Mecca ointment to carbolic acid, Mitch survived and concludes his true story by asking

—what I want to know is — here I am healthy and sound—how can it be after finishing all those medicines — there isn't a God, Owen.

[Act III, Sc. xliv]

This scene ends with Owen affirming his belief in God, and using the bottles that Mitch has brought along to illustrate his parable; to turn the stage red, yellow, blue. Magic in the ordinary, if examined sympathetically, is a theme running through the play from the title ("*listen* to the wind as if it were the only living thing in the world"), to the play-within-the-play, to the wash of color on the stage at this part of the third act. Owen's world seems to be slowly dying around him: he needs this sensitivity and belief.

If Geraldine has made herself, correctly or not, the vengeful Old Testament God of Caresfoot Court meting out stern and final judgement, Angela is the redemptive Christ-figure betrayed by "Judas" Piers. She is the miracle-maker kindly enough to weep for the scorpion and able to free Geraldine from the evil that has trapped her. Perhaps her greatest redemptive act is loving Arthur Brenzaida, who really *is* a weakling. Brenzaida, faced with the loss of Angela to Douglas, smashes dead a swan in a scene pointedly constructed to remind the audience of the young Piers in the garden with Claudia. As his ideal of a perfect woman shatters, Arthur engages in the howl of self-pity characteristic of Reaney's young heroes:

> . . . Was your lust for your cousin so strong that you could not wait till after I returned? When I think of the temptation I withstood — and I am a man. An older woman constantly by me, dreaming of my flesh . . . But I see now you were weaker than I and bubbled in March, no in January, like tar on a scorched July highway. . . .
>
> [Act III, Sc. xlv, xlvi, and xlvii]

Fortunately, the weakness of Arthur is balanced by the great strength of Angela, who recovers from her illness to reconcile herself with Geraldine and then in the ballroom dancing of the closing scene discovers herself to be Arthur's bride, contrary to her fears. Their marriage resolves the tensions in the Caresfoot/Lawry households, and the dance that ends the play connotes the return of civilization and order to the conflict and strife-torn world below in Caresfoot Court.

The world above in Perth County is gloomy and relieved only by the intense involvement of Owen and his friends in the play. For the first time, everyday life in Perth County is not paradisal in a Reaney play. Martha tells ghost stories; Mitch tries to cheer Owen up with ghoulish jokes about premature burial, and despite the location on the farm, the characters are only once connected with agriculture. The only animals mentioned as natural to the farm — the horses — are used as gambits in the bitter endgame Mr. and Mrs. Taylor are playing. In this sterile, half-macabre existence it seems natural for Mrs. Taylor to say: "I can't stand sickness and death. You gave me two children who died" [Act III, Sc. xlv, xlvi, and xlvii] or Owen to reveal that in choosing whether Angela should live or die, "I must confess when we drew the straws to see whether she would live or die I tipped the death one your way—ever so slightly.'' [Act III, Sc. xlv, xlvi, and xlvii]

Away from this world dominated by the dreams of a child, sick nearly to death, are the dreams, and Caresfoot Court. For me, the complexity arising from the attachment of these dreams and creative works to the subdued and muted realism of the Perth County sequences make *Listen to the Wind* the greatest of Reaney's plays. Through his efforts to enforce the transition from the sickly world above as it gives way to the civilized and playful world below, Reaney achieved an unusually forceful transformation of one reality to another. As the director of the play's 1966 premiere in London, Ontario, Reaney unquestionably became the true *auteur* of the production: selecting the material, casting some of the roles, working the chorus into precision, and encouraging the spontaneous variations that arise in a workshop atmosphere. The cohesion of the performances was remarkable, as Jay Macpherson notes:

> But where the Peking (Opera) company relies on the fantastic training and bodily control of its actors, what is astonishing in Reaney's production is the sense of play, of freedom, of creation before one's eyes. Far from being instant or impromptu theatre, every action has been carefully planned; but the whole company has contributed to its planning, particularly in the highly inventive work of the chorus.[10]

At the start of this section a note was made of the semiological nature of *Listen to the Wind*, and of the rare and complex interplay of textural levels in the work. The use of the chorus provides an example of this complexity. The chorus may produce quick sketches through sound and mime of the location of a scene; comment on the scene (Sc. xxxii, "the Eternity Chorus" and sc. xlix "We wove a web in Childhood") both raise the creativity inherent in the adaptation of *Dawn* to immortality in a way that direct speech by the characters could not approximate. They may be the schoolchildren in Ann's class years later putting on their snowsuits or a pack of ravenous dogs tearing apart Piers Caresfoot. The script of *Listen to the Wind* reflects this complexity in other areas. The concept of allowing the audience to observe the production of the play in progress is a modern, cognitive device to remind the audience that the play should be considered from a detached position. *Listen to the Wind* makes extensive use of this ability of modern theatre to examine the nature of theatre itself, but the result is not a detached, intellectual consideration of the play as a work of theatre criticism. A scene such as the primarily narrative (vii) "At the Edge of the Forest," includes a substantial diversity of similar material integrated naturally into several segments. The forest mime throughout the scene; the Geraldine/Douglas romance, as these young lovers are contrasted dramatically with the pairs of Piers/Claudia and Arthur/Angela; the entry of Geraldine into the play as the ambitious force capable of murdering her own child to clear the way forward; the introduction of Owen's mother into the play (a major moment for Owen and his friends . . . now that she is back, perhaps she'll stay?), and then her entry into the play-within-a-play in the whirling gesture (repeated later in *Sticks and Stones The Donnellys, Part One*); the ghost story which forms the murky bottom of the plot requiring a different pace and mood from the Geraldine/Douglas scenes or the Owen/Mrs. Taylor conversation. The chorus does not break this scene up with chants or poetry as elsewhere, but a full range of texts and codes are freely amalgamated throughout.

Instead of forcing us to notice that we are in an audience watching a play, this bold mixture of levels draws us further into the imaginative world of the Saga. So we find ourselves separate from the normal world in which people talk about marriage breakups, "melodrama," the problems of presenting a play, the sickness of a child. The effect of the transition from world to world is to make us a part of the fantastic and perfectly formed world below, the region of noble love, utter compelling evil, ruin and dance, and we rise like the fiddler from the bottom of society to the engagement ball. What the play keeps reminding us is that the way through our world of sickness and breakdown is play, which is the verb as well as the noun, action and thinking about action.

Notes to Chapter Ten

1. Barthes, Roland. "Literature and Signification" from *Critical Essays*, translated by Richard Howard, (Evanston: Northwestern University Press, 1972), pp. 261-62.

2. Reaney, James. *Listen to the Wind*, edited by Peter Hay, (Vancouver: Talonbooks, 1972). Unless noted otherwise, all references are drawn from this edition.

3. I find that the direct celebration of "melodrama," which is inherent in the dramatic adaptation of *Dawn* is best considered in light of the amused self-awareness that Reaney brings to the spectacular details of the Haggard novel. This kind of ironic attachment to bits of personal treasure and memory (the "playbox" again) is a unifying feature in his diverse career.

4. Brontë, Emily. *Wuthering Heights*, edited by William Sale Jr., (New York: W. W. Norton, 1963).

5. Brontë, Emily. *Wuthering Heights*, edited by William Sale Jr., (New York: W. W. Norton, 1963), p. 199.

6. Brontë, Emily. *Gondal's Queen: A Novel in Verse,* edited by Fanny Ratchford, (Austin: University of Texas Press, 1947).

7. Lee, Alvin A. *James Reaney*, (New York: Twayne Publishers, 1969), p. 152.

8. Parker, Brian. "Reaney and the Mask of Childhood" from *Masks of Childhood*, (Toronto, new press, 1972), p. 285.

9. The first image of the play is the ball-tossing, and while the ball seems to disappear from the farmhouse once the children find themselves immersed in the world below, I think that as they advance into the world around Caresfoot Court, the picture of Owen and the three girls tossing the yellow ball back and forth should be kept in mind as the children earnestly discuss their feelings about the characters, plot, production of "The Saga of Caresfoot Court." Tossing around the possibilities of Angela dying should be nearly as subtle or simple as playing catch with your friends: again, one kind of play is a part of the other.

10. Macpherson, Jay. "Preface" from *Listen to the Wind*, (Vancouver: Talonbooks, 1972), p. 8.

11

Conclusion: The One Big Play

Although his contributions, both as a theorist and a playwright have been gaining acceptance, James Reaney's work is still controversial. The growing acceptance of Reaney as an accomplished dramatist has been particularly noticeable in the approval of *Colours in the Dark*. Michael Tait, who summarized critical opinion of *The Killdeer* and *The Easter Egg* in 1964:

> I will concede, however, that of all Canadian dramatists, Reaney is the most difficult to evaluate justly. No one else has his capacity to write for the stage at once so badly and so well . . . [1]

wrote of *Colours in the Dark* eight years later:

> . . . Equally unimportant is the difficulty the play has given reviewers and critics. Reaney's creation is *sui generis*, a luminous structure that invites but eludes classification. It is lyric in subjective intensity and mood; dramatic in the articulation of larger conflicts; epic in its breadth of statement. Whatever the mode, the artist's transfiguring eye lights the scene and wrings a design from the ignorant chaos . . . [2]

To a considerable extent, the praise for *Colours in the Dark* or the later plays in general has been at the expense of the earlier works.[3]

Louis Dudek has delivered perhaps the strongest assertion of this position:

> For my own taste I could probably do without *The Killdeer*, *The Sun and the Moon*, *Three Desks*,—much as there may be interesting things in all of them—and I believe the best of Reaney's theatre pure symbolism in the romantic vein of Maeterlinck and Yeats is to be found in *Night-blooming Cereus*, *One-man Masque*, and the moving and impressive later plays *Listen to the Wind* and *Colours in the Dark*. It is here that he suggests vast meanings and haunting other-worldly dimensions through the simplest verbal and theatrical techniques, namely through the symbolic interplay of action and the incantation of poetry.[4]

On the other hand, Reaney's early theatre has been defended in no uncertain terms by Alvin Lee:

> His plays are not for cynics, nor for those too sophisticated to let themselves play games if necessary to exorcise the black enchantments laid on them in childhood. The measure in which we feel these resolutions silly, or too far-fetched is the measure of our own Malvolio-like nature . . . [5]

and more cautiously by Brian Parker:

> Too emphatic—too exclusive—a child's eye view sacrifices the mixture of "myth" and "documentary" which makes Act I of *Killdeer* still Reaney's most successful drama, and it weakens the complex relation with the audience which comes from our awareness of the dramatist's own presence . . . [6]

Now, in dividing the critics into these uneasy alliances, I have set them to shadow boxing rather unfairly. In the proper context the critics may be observed as reacting to one another. So, going backwards chronologically: Brian Parker is commenting upon Ross Woodman who is reflecting on Michael Tait who is replying to Alvin Lee who is challenging (probably) Nathan Cohen. Rather than chance a little shadow boxing on my own, I'd like to propose a new consideration of Reaney's drama: what the plays "mean," and "how" they mean it. While my own favorite of his plays is *Listen to the Wind* (technique over meaning), it isn't my intention to examine the plays for selection as good/bad or before/after. Throughout this book, I have tried to treat all the works as valuable—and with an artist such as Reaney who is capable of abrupt changes in direction, this is the safest procedure. Reaney has changed from poetry to drama, and from one kind of drama to another in the last fifteen years. Faced with these changes, it is the critic's job to adjust to the new developments and work with reference to the new artistic paradigms.

During the introduction, a kind of history was proposed as being necessary to record accurately the history of Canadian drama, and the story of James Reaney's plays. This history is the giant collection of all drama, giving everything, similar or dissimilar, equal consideration, and proceeding from there. For Reaney plays the method must be different. One must organize the great variety of material into a system of oppositions, similarities/dissimilarities that compose the one big play that Reaney keeps writing. Editing the plays together, one is able to discover the shape of the world in his dramas, and the underlying consistency of his concerns.

The universe in Reaney's theatre is divided into two groups, pitched in fundamental opposition. On the one hand are the good, the true, the just: (Dr. Ballad, Mr. Orchard, Francis Kingbird, Harry Gardner, Rebecca Lorimer, Jacob Waterman, Applebutter, Rev. Gleneden, Weathergood/Coyote, Rev.

Hackaberry, Angela Caresfoot, Pollex Henry, Ira Hill, Hilda History, Treewuzzle, Farmer Dell, Mrs. Soper, Bible Sal, concluding with the Donnellys). On the other hand are the forces of darkness: (Charlotte Shade, Victor Nipchopper, Linda Axmouth, Mr. Wolfwind, the Schoolmaster, Bethel Henry, Maximilian Niles, Madam Fay, Mr. Manatee, Clifford Hopkins, Thorntree, Lady Eldred, Douglas Caresfoot, Grizzly Bear, concluding with the Whitefeet). Any character such as Andrew Kingbird, Eli, George Sloan, Bill Thompson, or Edward Durelle who finds himself/herself in the forbidden zone between the two camps must choose sides, and once the choice is made, there is no turning back.

An immediate impression created by this division is that we have been invited into a naive, childish land where everything is neatly separated. There are beautiful names or ugly suspicious names. Characters are labelled either good or bad, never to contradict this label. Thorntree is cursed with a hateful nature, and is able to find peace with himself only as a real thorntree, and that is that.

Many critics have cited Reaney's religious upbringing as an explanation for his Manichean separation of characters into powers of light and darkness. One might call this the *Satan or Christ?* critical option, and I find myself at odds with it. The minority evangelical Protestantism of the Interdenominational Sunday School Reaney attended has undoubtedly influenced him profoundly. To give this factor pre-eminence, however, implies a critical determinism. Reproducing the atmosphere of Perth County in the plays naturally demands a depiction of the choice facing the child between shining good and sinister, alluring evil. Reaney is skilled at manipulating this small-town *persona*, and has kept the choice in perspective. Tension in his drama arises not so much in the conflict between the two camps—which is frequently left unresolved—but rather in the doubts and confusions of the characters in the middle. His plays are concerned with the necessity of making a choice and not simply with those who have already chosen.

The perspective that keeps the choice in focus for Reaney is the family. The conflict and doubt are placed in the confines of a farmhouse, a village, always tearing away at the family at its centre. As Reaney wrote in his thesis on the "Novels of Ivy Compton-Burnett":

In a way, what has struck me as being the most about Compton-Burnett's work is the indestructibility of the families she writes about in the face of the most destructive plots. . . . So many novelists describe wickedness in a sphere that does not really matter; Compton-Burnett is careful to place her evil and tyranny in a very vital arena, — The Family . . . [7]

Right down to the description of the family conflict as taking place in an "arena," this observation predicts the ambience of the dramas Reaney was to write. Think of the families, heroic, or demonic in his plays: the Lorimers, the Fays, Kingbirds, Moodys, Henrys, Taylors, Caresfoots, Almedas, Dells, Donnellys, Farls, Donegans, Thompsons. Reaney has followed Compton-Burnett's manner in locating his conflict and his good and bad characters in a family context. Instead of supposing that evil is a cosmic force in the plays, with Satan launching offensives all over the map (the "Satan or Christ?" manner), the arena is compact and the battle fought over seemingly trivial matters. Interestingly, *Three Desks* — called "unfortunate" by one critic — is the one play that does not concern the conflict within a family, or end with the beginning of a new family. Perhaps, in addition to the ironic affection of his Souwesto folk plays, Reaney also needs a strong family situation at the core of his plays to present fully his concerns and feelings.

Among previous critical works Alvin Lee, Ross Woodman, and Brian Parker have sensitively discussed the significance of childhood and maturity in Reaney's plays. Without downplaying the importance of this theme I'd like to continue thinking about the context of the child's growth to maturity, the family. Or more particularly parent/child relationships, since part of the child's struggle with innocence and experience narrates the search for spiritual "true" parents. The end of this odyssey is the key to Reaney's theatre. The denouement of *these plays* is a scene uniting the adult and the child, a summing up of the search and a prophecy of the future. For the most part these scenes are of reconciliation and recognition as the children and the "true parents" accept their new lives. Despite their differences *The Killdeer*, *The Easter Egg*, *The Sun and the Moon*, *Night-blooming Cereus*, *Names and Nicknames*, *One-man Masque*, *Geography Match*, *Applebutter*, *Colours in the Dark* all conclude in this fashion. Sometimes it is the child who initiates the reconciliation (*Applebutter*), and sometimes the patience and love of the adults (*The Killdeer* or *The Sun and the Moon*), and sometimes it is a combined effort (*Geography Match* or *Names and Nicknames*). Whatever the inspiration, the mood is one of optimism, new societies, healthiness. There is one satiric exception, *Ignoramus* (the founding of the perfect society is delayed a year in the tie-breaker) and one demonic exception, *Three Desks*. Jacob Waterman, the "parent" is forced to murder Niles to preserve the old society, sick as it is. The more sombre mood of *The Donnellys* is apparent in their closing scenes. *Sticks and Stones* finished with Jennie unable to convince her mother and father to leave Biddulph, even in dream. *The St. Nicholas Hotel* reaches a more ominously painful conclusion as Mrs. Donnelly soliloquizes by the coffin of her son Michael, the first of the family to be murdered by the Whitefeet. *Listen to the Wind* matches the optimism of the comedies with the foreboding of the Donnelly Trilogy. Owen fails to find his "true parents"; his mother and father do not reach out to prevent him from slipping away; but "The Saga of Caresfoot

Court'' ends optimistically. The ghost-child doll finds her ''true mother'' in Angela, and the play ends with the betrothal dance, so long delayed, of Angela and Arthur.

The steady recurrence of these closing scenes uniting parent and child in genres as different as *One-man Masque* and *Applebutter* indicates their importance to Reaney's drama. For Reaney, the child is not observed in isolation. The uncertain progress to maturity takes place in the definite context of the family, especially in the relations between the child and the parents. If, in Reaney's theatre, the child is the source of the divine innocence that allows the return to Eden in the fallen world, the family is also vital in the protection of the child. As the child moves from innocence to experience, wise and loving parents are needed to ensure that the child is safe from the dangers of false innocence (the inverted child) or too sudden an entry into the world of experience (the hateful and distorted childhood's of many of Reaney's villains). In the idealized families of Harry and Rebecca, or the Kingbirds, or even the Donnellys we see a little of what the return to Eden might resemble, both in the children and the adults.

Still, to me, the value of Reaney's work in the theatre is not so much in the plays' meanings, or the range of styles he has attempted. Rather, it lies in the social implications of his post-1966 theatre, particularly during the period when The Listener's Workshop was being held every Saturday morning. The challenge of *The Killdeer* was found in its ambitious conception and language: the audience was confronted with a new kind of theatre in Canada. *Listen to the Wind* and the workshop challenged the conception of ''the theatre'' in a radical way best summarized by another London artist:

> . . . It is also interesting to consider that John Cage has compared himself to the camera manufacturer (which is the position that Reaney has put himself in)[8] and that the other notable (and for me valid) use of amateurs that comes to mind is ''the happening'' and some of them . . . are autobiographical. They are also very regional. Finally consider that parents can, and probably will, go to see their children be in Jamie's plays in the same way that they go to see them play in a pee wee hockey game.[9]

Reaney has moved away from this spontaneous theatre in his Donnelly plays, writing specific parts with the dramatic abilities of certain members of the Tarragon cast in mind. Further, he has spoken of the ideal situation in the theatre as comparable to the commedia dell'arte, with a stock company of trained actors fully skilled in their roles as special character types. It may be that his work with the Tarragon company will allow him to fulfill his ambition of continuing the development of his theatre in a new direction. If this is indeed the case, *The Donnellys* may be only a hint of the plays James Reaney has yet to write, and its dense, precise style will be the way of his future.

To my own mind, however, Reaney's masterpiece and his greatest contribution to the Canadian theatre will remain *Listen to the Wind*. Reaney's consolidation of meaning, technique, chance, order, personality and universality, as avant garde as John Cage and as intrinsically Canadian as pee wee hockey transforms Play into "play," the theatre into our lives.

Notes to Chapter Eleven

1. Tait, Michael. "The Limits of Innocence" from *Dramatists in Canada*, edited by William New, (Vancouver: University of British Columbia Press, 1972), p. 139.

2. Tait, Michael. "Everything is Something" from *Dramatists in Canada*, edited by William New, (Vancouver: University of British Columbia Press, 1972), p. 144.

3. Ross Woodman has pointed out that the opulent production that *Colours in the Dark* received in its 1967 première at Stratford's Avon Theatre is somewhat odd in the context of Reaney's career.

4. Dudek, Louis. "A Problem of Meaning" from *Canadian Literature* No. 59, (Winter, 1974), p. 28.

5. Lee, Alvin. "A Turn to the Stage" from *Dramatists in Canada*, edited by William New, (Vancouver, University of British Columbia Press, 1972), p. 132.

6. Parker, Brian. "Reaney and the Mask of Childhood" from *Masks of Childhood*, edited by Brian Parker (Toronto, new press, 1972), p. 289.

7. Reaney, James. "The Novels of Ivy Compton-Burnett", M.A. Thesis, (University of Toronto, 1949), p. 4.

8. "Four years ago John Hirsch directed one of my children's plays, *Names and Nicknames*, at the Manitoba Theatre Centre. With a dozen children, six young actors (among them, Martha Henry and Heath Lambert) and words taken from my father's old *Practical Speller*, John Hirsch created a magic hour that has remained with me ever since. The simpler art is — the richer it is. Words, gestures, a few rhythm band instruments create a world that turns Cinerama around and makes you the movie projector." Reaney, James. "Production Notes: 1966" from *Listen to the Wind*, edited by Peter Hay, (Vancouver: Talonbooks, 1972), p. 117.

9. Curnoe, Greg. "Letters to the Editor" from *Twenty Cents Magazine* Vol. I, No. 4, (December 1966), p. 5.

Bibliography

James Reaney

Plays and Dramatic Writing:

"The Rules of Joy," 1958.

"The Revenger's Tragedie by Cyril Tourneur," (adaptation), 1961.

The Killdeer and Other Plays. Toronto: Macmillan of Canada, 1962. This collection contains *The Killdeer*, *The Sun and the Moon*, *One-man Masque*, and *Night-blooming Cereus*, with John Beckwith.

Poet and City — Winnipeg with John Beckwith, from *Poetry 62*, edited by Eli Mandel and Jean-Guy Pilon. Toronto: The Ryerson Press, 1962.

"Wednesday's Child," with John Beckwith, 1962.

"Euripides' Bacchae,"(adaptation), 1963.

Let's Make a Carol: A Play with Music, with Alfred Kunz. Waterloo: Waterloo Music Company, 1965.

"The Shivaree," with John Beckwith, 1965.

"Little Red Riding Hood," 1965.

"Part One, Canada Dash, Canada Dot: The Line Across," with John Beckwith, 1965.

"Part Two, Canada Dash, Canada Dot: The Line Up and Down," with John Beckwith, 1965-66.

"Don't Sell Mr. Aesop," 1967.

"Genesis," 1967.

Names and Nicknames from *Nobody in the Cast*, edited by R. Barton, D. Booth *et al*. Toronto: Longman Canada Limited, 1969.

Colours in the Dark. Vancouver: Talonbooks, 1969.

Listen to the Wind. Vancouver: Talonbooks, 1972.

Masks of Childhood, edited by Brian Parker. Toronto: new press, 1972. This collection contains *The Easter Egg*, *Three Desks*, and a revised edition of *The Killdeer*.

"Some Dramatic Verse 1953-71," from *Poems*, edited by Germaine Warkentin. Toronto: new press, 1972. This section contains selections from *Nightblooming Cereus* with John Beckwith, *The Killdeer* (1972), "Euripides' *Bacchae*," "Canada Dash, Canada Dot, Part Two: The Line Up and Down" with John Beckwith, *Listen to the Wind*, Colours in the Dark, and *Donnelly*.

Applebutter and Other Plays for Children. Vancouver: Talonbooks, 1973. This collection contains *Applebutter*, *Geography Match*, *Names and Nicknames*, and *Ignoramus*.

"The St. Nicholas Hotel The Donnellys, Part Two," 1974.

"Handcuffs The Donnellys, Part Three," 1975.

Sticks and Stones The Donnellys, Part One. Erin: Press Porcépic, 1975.

Poetry:

The Red Heart. Toronto: McClelland & Stewart, 1949.

A Suit Of Nettles. Toronto: Macmillan of Canada, 1958; Erin: Press Porcépic, 1975.

Twelve Letters to a Small Town. Toronto: The Ryerson Press, 1962.

The Dance of Death at London, Ontario with Jack Chambers. London: The Alphabet Press, 1963.

Poems, edited by Germaine Warkentin. Toronto: new press, 1972.

Selected Shorter Poems edited by Germaine Warkentin. Erin: Press Porcépic, 1975.

Selected Fiction:

"The Box-Social," *The Undergrad* (1947), pp. 30-31; *New Liberty Magazine*, XXIV (July 19, 1947).

"Afternoon Moon," 1948.

"The Young Necrophiles," *Canadian Forum*, XXVIII (September 1948), pp. 136-37.

"The Bully," from *Canadian Short Stories*, edited by Robert Weaver and Helen James. Toronto: Oxford University Press, 1952; *Canadian Short Stories*, edited by Robert Weaver. London: Oxford University Press, 1960.

"Dear Metronome," *Canadian Forum*, XXXII (September 1952), pp. 134-37.

"Winnipeg Sketches," *Canadian Forum*, XXXV (November 1955), pp. 175-76.

The Boy with an R in his Hand. Toronto: Macmillan of Canada, 1965.

Selected Non-fiction:

"The Novels of Ivy Compton-Burnett," Master's thesis, University of Toronto, 1949.

"The Plays at Stratford," *Canadian Forum*, XXXIII (September 1953), pp. 134-35.

"The Canadian Poets Predicament," *University of Toronto Quarterly*, XXVI

(April 1957), pp. 284-85; *Masks of Poetry: Canadian Critics on Canadian Verse*, edited by A.J.M. Smith. Toronto: McClelland and Stewart, 1962.

"The Influence of Spenser on Yeats," Doctoral thesis, University of Toronto, 1958.

"The Canadian Imagination," *Poetry* (Chicago), XCIV (June 1959), pp. 186-89.

Alphabet: A Semiannual Devoted to the Iconography of the Imagination, edited by James Reaney. vols. 1-20. London, 1960-71.

"An Evening with Babble and Doodle: Presentations of Poetry," *Canadian Literature*, XII (Spring, 1962), pp. 37-43.

"E.J. Pratt: The Dragonslayer," in *Great Canadians*, edited by Pierre Berton *et al*. Toronto: The Great Centennial Publishing Company, 1965.

"Ten Years at Play," *Canadian Literature*, XLI (Summer, 1969, pp. 53-61.

"James Reaney's Canada: The Poetic Rubbings of a Defensive Driver," *Maclean's Magazine*, (December 1971), pp. 18-19, 46.

"Donnelly, James," entry in *Dictionary of Canadian Biography* X, pp. 23-4-35. Toronto: University of Toronto Press, 1972.

"Myths in Some Nineteenth Century Newspapers," from *Aspects of Nineteenth Century Ontario*, edited by F.H. Armstrong *et al*. Toronto: University of Toronto Press, 1974.

"Some Questions and Some Answers," 1975.

Selected Criticism:

Cohen, Nathan. "Mr. Reaney Writes a Play," *Toronto Daily Star*, January 14, 1960.

Dudek, Louis. "A Problem of Meaning," *Canadian Literature*, LIX, (Winter 1974), pp. 16-39.

Klinck, C.F. (General Editor). *Literary History of Canada: Canadian Literature in English*. Toronto: University of Toronto Press, 1965, pp. 648-49.

Kraglund, John, "An Experiment in Lyric Theatre," *The Globe and Mail*, April 6, 1960.

Lee, Alvin A. "A Turn to the Stage: Reaney's Dramatic Verse," *Canadian Literature* , XVXVI (Winter, 1963) and (Spring, 1963), pp 40-51 and pp. 41-53.

Lee, Alvin A. *James Reaney*. New York: Twayne Publishers, 1969.

Macpherson, Jay. "Listen to the Wind," *Canadian Forum*, XLVI (September 1966), pp. 136-37.

Moore, Mavor. "This Play May Become Part of Our History." *Toronto Telegram* January 27, 1960.

Moore, Mavor. *Four Canadian Playwrights: Robertson Davies, Gratien Gélinas, James Reaney, George Ryga*. Toronto: Holt, Rinehart and Winston, 1973.

Parker, Brian. "Reaney and the Mask of Childhood," from *Masks of Childhood*. Toronto: new press, 1972.

Tait, Michael. "The Limits of Innocence: James Reaney's Theatre," *Canadian Literature*, XIX (Winter, 1964), pp. 43-48.

Tait, Michael. "Everything is Something: James Reaney's *Colours in the Dark*" from *Dramatists in Canada: Selected Essays*, edited by William New. Vancouver: University of British Columbia Press, 1972.

Warkentin, Germaine. "The Artist in Labour: James Reaney's Plays," *Journal of Canadian Fiction*, Vol. 2, No. 1 (Winter, 1973), pp. 88-91.

Water, Esther. "Crime and No Punishment," *Canadian Literature* XLIX (Summer, 1971), pp. 55-60.

Whittaker, Herbert. "Cast Copes with *Killdeer* Difficulties," *The Globe and Mail*, October 18, 1974.

Wilson, Milton. "On Reviewing Reaney," *The Tamarack Review*, XXVI (Winter, 1963), pp. 71-78.

Woodman, Ross G. *James Reaney*. Toronto: McClelland and Stewart, 1972.

Zimmer, Elizabeth. *Listen to the Wind*, *The Fourth Estate*, January 25, 1973.

Index